MW00954868

Breakable Bond

DIANE STEINER

ARCHWAY
PUBLISHING

Copyright © 2015 Diane Steiner.

All rights reserved. No part of this book may be used or reproduced by any means, graphic, electronic, or mechanical, including photocopying, recording, taping or by any information storage retrieval system without the written permission of the publisher except in the case of brief quotations embodied in critical articles and reviews.

Archway Publishing books may be ordered through booksellers or by contacting:

Archway Publishing
1663 Liberty Drive
Bloomington, IN 47403
www.archwaypublishing.com
1 (888) 242-5904

Because of the dynamic nature of the Internet, any web addresses or links contained in this book may have changed since publication and may no longer be valid. The views expressed in this work are solely those of the author and do not necessarily reflect the views of the publisher, and the publisher hereby disclaims any responsibility for them.

Any people depicted in stock imagery provided by Thinkstock are models, and such images are being used for illustrative purposes only.
Certain stock imagery © Thinkstock.

ISBN: 978-1-4808-1676-3 (sc)
ISBN: 978-1-4808-1386-1 (hc)
ISBN: 978-1-4808-1675-6 (e)

Library of Congress Control Number: 2015905261

Print information available on the last page.

Archway Publishing rev. date: 07/06/2015

Introduction

The story of Joshua and Ahmed is about a serendipitous friendship—one that develops accidently despite a long-held conflict between the Palestinian and Israeli people. It is through a devastating circumstance that these two boys become friends. This story of friendship could continue between the Israeli and Palestinian people each and every day if given a chance.

Ahmed came from the Palestinian city of Tulkarm, situated on the western part of the northern West Bank. It sits in the foothills of the Samarian Mountains and is about nine miles east of the lovely and popular Israeli coastal town of Netanya. Ahmed's grandparents and parents grew up here and earned their living tending to the vineyards, which produced an abundance of citrus fruits. In the summer, Ahmed loved to help his Abi (father) and jiddo (grandfather) gather the fruit to be sold in the marketplace. He would carefully separate the oranges, lemons, and dates into baskets and stack them in his father's truck to drive to market in town. Ahmed would also ride with his Abi to the checkpoint to bring his produce for sale in Netanya.

As much as Ahmed enjoyed helping his family, he became fearful of the marketplace. In December, many people had been

صداقة ידידות صداقة ידידות صداقة ידידות صداقة ידידות

killed and injured when an explosive went off as a bomber exited a taxicab. An Israeli soldier and several Palestinians had been the victims of this attack. When Ahmed talked to his Abi about his fears, his Abi would reply, "Ahmed, we must go on living. We have to eat, so we must sell our fruit. Be patient, the world will get better." Ahmed had faith in his Abi's words, but not in the world he lived in.

Joshua was an Israeli boy who lived in the seashore city of Netanya. It was a beautiful city with a breathtaking coastline. Many French and Russian Jewish immigrants, as well as a small group of Ethiopian Jews, settled and vacationed in this city. Joshua's saba (grandfather) owned a store that sold beautiful handmade, woven carpets. Joshua's Aba (father) inherited the business, and he used to have many Palestinian customers who purchased carpets and prayer rugs for their homes. They had been devoted customers for many years. When the Green Line—a security wall—was created by Israel, the opportunity for Palestinians to work, shop, or trade in Netanya became limited.

On the days when Joshua had nothing to do, he would visit his Aba's store and help out, but the store's business was not as prosperous as it had once been. The large, modern department stores carried a large selection of rugs and carpeting at prices that Joshua's Aba could not compete with. It was only a matter of time before he would close his store.

Joshua helped out of respect for his Aba, but it wasn't something he enjoyed doing. In a few weeks, he would be working on his soccer game at an Israeli camp he attended every summer. Joshua was very disturbed about the recent bombings at the shopping mall and

صداقة يديدوت صداقة يديدوت صداقة يديدوت صداقة يديدوت

could not understand why some people wanted to harm or kill other people. He and his Aba had many discussions about the problems between the Palestinians and Israelis, but these discussions always ended without a satisfying solution.

صداقة يديدوت صداقة يديدوت صداقة يديدوت صداقة يديدوت

Chapter 1

Ahmed wiped his brow. He couldn't seem to stay cool with the heavy moisture in the air. This was unusual weather in Tulkarm. Even though it was usually hot this time of year, the atmosphere seemed to be exploding with dampness. Ahmed was looking forward to a game of soccer with his friends. They were practicing for a competition to be held in two weeks.

"Are you sure, Abi, that you will not need me to help bring the fruit to market?" Ahmed asked.

"You have been a great help to me and Jiddo. You, Ahmed, have earned a day of play. Go have fun, but practice to win!" Ahmed's Abi was a serious man who often put his work first, but what was most important to him was the well-being of his family. He knew how much soccer meant to Ahmed, and secretly he was hoping his son would become the champion soccer player that he never became.

Ahmed had many dreams of playing in the great Al-Khader Stadium, and he kept this dream close to his heart. He felt sure that if he practiced hard enough, his dream would come true one day.

Ahmed met his friend Mahmoud and some other boys to get ready for the game. When Mahmoud saw Ahmed coming

صداقة يديدות صداقة يديدות صداقة يديدות صداقة يديدות

toward him, he yelled out to him, "Have you heard what happened, Ahmed?"

"About what, Mahmoud? Catch your breath and tell me the news."

"Some Israeli soldiers came to my house and told my father that he had four weeks to gather our belongings and leave. My Abi didn't know I was listening, and he hasn't told me anything about it. I'm really angry, Ahmed. These soldiers are heartless; they would love to demolish more than the houses. My Abi's family built our house. I have known nothing else. What will my family do?"

Ahmed hesitated and put his arm around his friend. "Your Abi is smart. He will figure something out. Maybe you will go live with other family members in another city. Don't worry. If you'd like, I will ask my Abi if you and your family can stay with us for a while."

"No, no, Ahmed, don't say anything. My Abi would feel so ashamed; he is a very proud man. Your offer is generous and you are truly a good friend, but promise me you will not say anything to him or anyone else. Promise?"

"Of course. If you need anything, I will do what I can to help you."

"I am so angry because the Israeli government expects our people to leave the only homes they have ever known. The little we have they want to take away from us. Be careful, Ahmed. It's only a matter of time before your family gets that knock on the door."

Ahmed could see the frustration on Mahmoud's face, and he wanted him to know that it was not all Israeli people who felt this way; however, this was not the time to explain this to him.

صداقة يديدות صداقة يديدות صداقة يديدות صداقة يديدות

صداقة يديدوت صداقة يديدوت صداقة يديدوت صداقة يديدوت

"Yes, Mahmoud, I will be careful, but everything will work out, you'll see."

"I hope you're right."

Ahmed sensed there were more important things to do now than playing soccer. Mahmoud seemed to think the same thing as he said, "I think it would be best if I stay here and wait for my Abi to come home. I think my Ommy, brothers, and sisters may need me. I hope you understand."

"Yes, I do understand, too clearly. Have you told anyone else?"

"Yes, Daoud came earlier, and I told him to tell the others that my family needed my help. That is all I told him. Good-bye, Ahmed," Mahmoud said sadly.

Ahmed sensed it would be the last time he would see his friend for a long time, but his concern was growing as he realized his family could be next. The family home was close to where the wall would be built, but was it too close? Close enough for the Israeli army to demolish it? At this time, there was no answer to his question. All he could do was wait patiently.

As Ahmed walked home, he thought about the continuing conflict between the Palestinians and the Israelis. He strongly believed that there could be a shared humanity between them and an appreciation and respect for each other.

"If only the common people could talk to one another and make the decisions, then maybe we would have a peaceful coexistence," Ahmed muttered hopefully. From his conversations with his Abi, he knew that when the conflict was left to governments and political groups, there would never be peace. Yet somehow, in his soul, he believed it could happen.

صداقة يديدوت صداقة يديدوت صداقة يديدوت صداقة يديدوت

صداقة يديدوت صداقة يديدوت صداقة يديدوت صداقة يديدوت

As he continued walking, he looked up to see clouds covering what had been a sunny, blue sky. He suddenly felt anxious as he thought about what happened to Mahmoud. *What if the same thing happens to my family? Where would we go? I must speak to Abi when I get home.* His pace quickened until he felt himself running toward home.

صداقة يديدوت صداقة يديدوت صداقة يديدوت صداقة يديدوت

Chapter 2

As he approached his house, Ahmed felt a calm come over him as he watched his Ommy and sister in the courtyard gathering the wash.

"Ahmed, you're home early. Didn't you have soccer practice with Mahmoud?"

"Yes, Ommy, but Mahmoud had a family emergency and had to cancel." His Ommy had a concerned look on her face and went back to her wash. "Where is Abi? Is he still at the marketplace?" Ahmed asked earnestly.

"You know he won't be back until late afternoon. It seems you need something to do. Here, hang the rest of the wash out to dry. When you finish that, I'll have more to take your mind off of whatever it is that is bothering you."

"But Ommy—"

"Never mind, just get this chore done. It will be a help to me," Ommy scolded.

With each piece of wash Ahmed hung up, he became more restless and wished his Abi would return home early. He thought about going to the marketplace after he finished his chores, and then he decided he didn't want his family to be suspicious of his intentions. *I'll be patient and speak to Abi after dinner.*

That was always the time when Ahmed and his Abi would have serious discussions about the world. The two of them seemed so close during those times, and it made Ahmed feel like a man. He worked on his chores and waited for dinner. Ahmed thought he heard the quiet footsteps of someone enter the house. He came running to see who it was and found his Abi slumped in a chair with his eyes half opened.

"Abi," Ahmed said apologetically, "are you all right? Can I get you some coffee?"

Yet Abi did not answer. As Ahmed was about to speak again, his Ommy came in with some nourishment of dried fruit and a cup of strong coffee. Her hand to her mouth, she motioned for Ahmed to go to his room. He looked puzzled and worried because his Abi usually came home energetic after a day of meeting customers and selling his goods in the marketplace.

He went to his room and moved close to the door so he would not miss any conversation between his parents. For what seemed like forever, there was silence, and then he heard his Abi speaking in a rapid-fire voice. Ahmed could sense the frustration in his voice. He could hear parts of the conversation and knew it was about the security wall being built. There had been several violent attacks on innocent people, both Palestinians and Israelis, and the Israeli government was beginning to erect barriers around the village of Tulkarm.

Abi's voice grew louder, and Ommy tried to calm him down. "You don't know what they will do. I fear—no, I *know* they will come in and bulldoze our home. Mahmoud's family has been told to leave, and I have spoken to others today who have been given

صداقة يديدوت صداقة يديدوت صداقة يديدوت صداقة يديدوت

the same warning. I am sure we will be next. Our home is close to where the wall will be built."

Ommy was upset but told her husband that they could stay with family. Abi did not want to hear this. All he knew was that the house he and Jiddo had built would be destroyed, and the life they once knew would be gone. At that moment, Ahmed heard the door open again and saw his jiddo mumbling to himself. He saw Abi walk toward Jiddo and attempt to put his arm around him.

Ahmed's jiddo pushed his son away and was frantically speaking in Arabic. Abi reached out to embrace him to slow his rapid speech, but he was unsuccessful. Ahmed tried to listen to what was being said, but he couldn't understand the message between the two. Then he carefully put his hand on the door and moved it gently to close it. *Tomorrow is another day,* he thought. *Abi will think of a solution.*

Ahmed waited a few minutes and then proceeded to get washed for prayers and dinner. He sat on the floor with his sister and played a game of marbles.

"Ahmed, can I ask you something?" his sister, Ayat, asked.

"Of course, what is it? You seem troubled?"

"Do you think we will have to leave our home? I have been hearing Ommy and Abi talking about it."

"I will not lie to you, Ayat. The Israeli government has given a warning to families whose homes are close to the barrier they are building. They say these families must gather their possessions and find another place to live." Ahmed whispered this to his sister for fear that one of his parents may hear him.

Ayat's body grew stiff, and her almond-shaped, black eyes grew

صداقة يديدوت صداقة يديدوت صداقة يديدوت صداقة يديدوت

صداقة يديدوت صداقة يديدوت صداقة يديدوت صداقة يديدوت

wider. The playfulness of the game began to take on a serious tone. "Don't worry, Ayat. Abi wouldn't let that happen to us. Now let's continue our game."

"Come, Ahmed, Ayat, it is time for prayers and then we will eat," called Ommy. "Please come and join us."

Ahmed joined his Abi and jiddo, while Ayat went beside her Ommy. The sajjada (prayer mats) were set down on the floor in the direction of Mecca. The prayers—salat—were recited, and then Ahmed and his father took the sajjada and put one on top of the other, covering them until the next prayers at dawn.

Ahmed and Ayat sat down on the cushions as their mother placed a platter of musakhan, a roasted chicken dish, along with taboon bread on the table. Ommy then came in with a bowl of spicy freekeh soup and maglaba. Ahmed felt something was different. His mother worked hard to put good food on the table, but there were dishes tonight that were saved for special occasions. That thought quickly changed with the aromas that came from his mother's kitchen, which comforted Ahmed and made him feel safe.

Today that feeling was short-lived because of the rumors he had heard. Jiddo and Abi sat opposite them. "Ommy, this is my favorite meal. Thank you." Ahmed then gulped down a glass of apricot juice. He wished his life would always be like this, content and well fed. During the meal, there was a loud banging on the door. His Abi rose and opened it ever so slightly. Ahmed could see nothing but his Abi walking outside and closing the door behind him. He went to get up, and his mother put her arm out to prevent him from rising.

A few moments later, the door closed and Abi walked back with

صداقة يديدوت صداقة يديدوت صداقة يديدوت صداقة يديدوت

صداقة ידידות صداقة ידידות صداقة ידידות صداقة ידידות

a stern look in his eyes as he returned to the table without saying a word. After several minutes he said, "Just a beggar looking for food. I gave him some fruit and nuts that I had left over from the market. Now, continue to enjoy this wonderful meal your Ommy has prepared for us." Ahmed could sense Abi was putting on the best acting role of his life, and yet he couldn't be entirely sure. His eyes met his jiddo's, staring intently for a moment, and then they both turned away.

After dinner, Ahmed retreated to his room and sat buried in his thoughts. *What if I wake up and I find out we are moving? Where will we go? It will never be the same as our house wherever it is.* Ahmed kept tossing and turning, asking himself one question after another, never having a satisfying answer. He finally wore himself out and drifted off to sleep, waking to bright sunshine. His eyes strained from trying to shield them from the sun. He could hear the sounds of dishes and smelled the aroma of strong coffee coming from the kitchen.

"In a few years, Ahmed," his Abi had told him, "you will join me for coffee." Ahmed couldn't wait a few years, so when he could, he would sneak a few sips of the deliciously dark and aromatic fluid. After all, in his house, like many other Palestinian homes, coffee would be made throughout the day. It was too hard to resist. Ahmed realized it was time for prayers and ran inside to find his family kneeling. He didn't understand why Ayat or any of his family had not woken him, and with that, he knelt down on his rug and began his prayers.

Life went on, and the day's routines remained uneventful: Abi and Jiddo going to market to sell their goods, Ommy taking care of

صداقة ידידות صداقة ידידות صداقة ידידות صداقة ידידות

صداقة ידידות صداقة ידידות صداقة ידידות صداقة ידידות

the home and preparing the evening meal for their return, and Ayat helping. Many weeks had passed quickly since that night. Another day was beginning for the Quessem family.

One day, Ahmed awoke and went to wash and get dressed for the day as he usually did. As he looked into the mirror, he said to himself that this was going to be the best day ever because he would make it so. The sun was shining, the coffee brewing, he was in a home with parents and a grandfather who loved him—what more could he ask?

As he walked toward the kitchen, his Ommy was leaning over the bowl making maqluba (an upside-down rice casserole) and a baked eggplant casserole for the evening's meal. Ayat was at the table eating an orange. She looked up and stared into Ahmed's eyes, looking as though she was about to say something but didn't.

"Good morning, Ommy and Ayat," Ahmed greeted them cheerfully. He looked around and noticed the absence of his father and grandfather. "Where are Abi and Jiddo?"

"They had a lot of business to do at the market today. Now sit down and eat. I need you to do an errand for me, and then I must leave to visit Khala Selima." She was Ahmed's mother's sister and his favorite aunt. There was some urgency in his Ommy's voice, but he was hesitant to question her.

"Okay, Ommy, what errand do I need to go on?"

"Do you know the apartment building a few miles from here going north? We have passed it many times. You must walk beyond the marketplace; and it is located on a hill. Please deliver this letter to the manager in charge. Do not leave until you get an answer from him. Do you understand? *You must leave with an answer.*"

صداقة ידידות صداقة ידידות صداقة ידידות صداقة ידידות

صداقة ידידות صداقة ידידות صداقة ידידות صداقة صداقة ידידות

"Ommy, you're frightening me. What is going on?" he asked with a quiver in his voice.

"Ahmed, don't ask questions, just do as I ask. Trust me to do what is right."

"Yes, Ommy, of course."

"Now, you are late for your prayers. When you finish, come and have something to eat. I have to go. I will see you later." She put her arms around him and squeezed him tight, nuzzling her cheek against his. "You are a good son, Ahmed, a jewel." He noticed her eyes beginning to get moist.

"Go, Ommy," Ahmed reassured her. "I'll see you later." He held the envelope tightly to his chest, handling it as though it were a piece of fine gold.

Ahmed went into the other room to put the sajjada on the floor to begin his morning prayer ritual. He noticed they were missing and searched the room with his eyes. Maybe Ommy had to move them, but she would have told him. *Something isn't right,* he thought. The dutiful son that he was, he knelt down on the floor and began his prayers, and then did as his Ommy had asked and had something to eat. He had a few spoonfuls then he grabbed the envelope and made sure he had identification with him, just in case he was stopped by someone. After this, he left the house.

As Ahmed walked, he passed the many olive groves of Tulkarm and actually enjoyed the intense heat of the morning. Except for the crumbling buildings that needed repair and the poverty he witnessed as he walked, he could see beyond this to the beauty that was Tulkarm. *This is a beautiful town,* he thought, *even more beautiful today.*

صداقة ידידות صداقة ידידות صداقة ידידות صداقة ידידות

صداقة ידידות صداقة ידידות صداقة ידידות صداقة ידידות

He picked up his pace as he greeted neighbors he had known since his early childhood. *This is further than I remember,* but just as he thought that and walked well past the marketplace, he could see the apartment building on the hill in the distance as his Ommy had described.

The building was situated along with several houses nearby. The whitewashed buildings were huddled together with barely any space between them, and the rooftops were irregular, looking like steps of different heights. Adults and children were everywhere, crowding among one another. Every few feet, women sat on benches made from scrap wood. Young boys attempted to play soccer in the narrow road separating the buildings. Squeezed into all of this were some shopkeepers calling out their prices.

He didn't know the contents of the envelope and was nervous thinking about the need for an answer from the manager. The area was busy with people having coffee and passionate discussions, yelling back and forth to get their points heard in order to convince their companions. Ahmed hesitated and then approached the steps to the apartment building.

A man was standing on the steps at the top gazing down at Ahmed with a vacant look in his eyes as if to say, "Who are you? You don't come from this village. Go away." His jacket was tattered and torn, and he wore no shoes. The man smiled at Ahmed as he reached the top step.

"Are you looking for someone?" the man said as he moved closer to Ahmed. He took a step away from the man as the strong smell of cigarette smoke came blowing through his fingers where a cigarette dangled.

صداقة ידידות صداقة ידידות صداقة ידידות صداقة ידידות

صداقة يدِيدوت صداقة يدِيدوت صداقة يدِيدوت صداقة يدِيدوت

"Yes, I need to see the manager. Is he here today?"

"Oh, you are a businessman," the man said sarcastically, "and you are planning to buy the building, yes?"

Ahmed was nervous and not in the mood for a joke-making ne'er-do-well. "Is he here? If you don't know, I'll go in to find him myself. This is urgent." As irritated as Ahmed was becoming, he was trying to be polite.

"Well, my good young man, I am the manager, and you are?"

"My name is Ahmed Quessem, and my Ommy wanted me to give this to you." He handed over the envelope and continued, "My Ommy said I can't leave without an answer."

"Oh, I see. Then an answer you will have. I am Moussa, young man." The man's eyes darted back and forth as he read Ahmed's Ommy's request. He then scribbled something on the paper and asked Ahmed to wait a moment for his return. A few minutes passed, and the man returned to Ahmed a newly sealed envelope.

"Mr. Quessem, you must hurry home as fast as you can. This information is very important to your Ommy. It was a pleasure doing business with you."

"Thank you, Mr. Moussa."

Chapter 3

Ahmed began running and felt a panic take over his body. Then he started breathing heavily and lost his strength. He fell to the ground, jumped back up, and stopped to catch his breath. *I wish I knew what was in this envelope. What could be so important? When did my Ommy meet Mr. Moussa?* His mind was racing with as many ideas as he could take in. His pace began to slow to a brisk walk.

Suddenly he realized it was midday, and he dropped his knees to the ground and began his prayers. *Our family will be all right, insh'allah, if God wills it,* he prayed. Ahmed was still out of breath and pushed his weary body to continue the path home. The sun and its intensity painted beads of sweat across his brow and neck. He was thirsty, and he opened and closed his parched mouth to keep it from sticking.

He stopped abruptly and blinked his eyes several times, then began rubbing them. "Did I go the wrong way? No, this is my neighborhood ... but it can't be, because I don't see my house."

As Ahmed got closer, he bent down to pick up some olives. As he continued to walk, he noticed a team of Israeli soldiers and then heard the sound of a bulldozer in the distance. He began running in circles, screaming as loud as he could. The Israeli soldiers turned to look at Ahmed briefly, and then went about the job they were sent to do, keeping things secure as the demolition of houses was

صداقة يديدوت صداقة يديدوت صداقة يديدوت صداقة يديدوت

completed. The house demolitions were the fate of the Palestinians whose homes had been built too close to the wall being erected.

Sitting on the dirt at a distance from his home and with the intensity of the sun still hovering over him, Ahmed tried to think clearly about what he was now witnessing. The big question remained for him, *Where is my family? There is nothing left of our possessions—did they have a chance to take anything with them? Were they forced to flee with only the clothes they wore?*

There were so many unanswered questions, and the only way to find the answers was to find his family. He decided to walk into the marketplace to find anyone he knew who could give him any information to help him find his family. *Asking the Israeli soldiers was a waste of time, he thought. They'd probably take me away.*

Ahmed was hungry and tired, and there was no one he knew in the immediate area near where once stood his home. He began a slow walk to the market and when he arrived, he saw groups of men speaking rapidly with their hands flying up in the air and their eyes wild and on fire. He recognized one of the merchants, Mr. Massoud, who was a friend of his father's. Mr. Massoud met Ahmed's eyes and called to him. Tears came running down Ahmed's face as he ran to the man.

"Mr. Massoud, my house is gone and so is my family. Do you know what happened and where they are? *I have nothing but my identification papers, nothing.* I am alone in the world, Mr. Massoud, *do you hear?*"

"Please, Ahmed, calm down. Everything happened so quickly. No one was given but a few weeks to collect their belongings. I don't know where your family is, but I do know this. They will come

صداقة يديدوت صداقة يديدوت صداقة يديدوت صداقة يديدوت

صداقة ידידות صداقة ידידות صداقة ידידות صداقة ידידות

back and find you, I promise," said Mr. Massoud in a consoling voice. "Come and sit down. I will give you something to eat and drink. You look like you've been on a reckless journey. You need to rest."

Ahmed was grateful for Mr. Massoud's kindness, and he felt his body relax. He would now look forward to the nuts and fruit to nourish him, than he would proceed with a plan. Maybe he would go to Netanya. He had heard so many stories from his father about the beautiful ocean and the shops, especially the mall.

Netanya was not an easy place for Palestinians to visit. Ever since the bombing at the mall, it was difficult, if not impossible, for Palestinians to get past the checkpoint. Ahmed would try anyway. He had his papers for the checkpoint. He had nothing to lose for he felt he had lost everything that was ever important to him. Ahmed felt confused and frightened but not enough to keep him from traveling to Netanya.

Mr. Massoud brought out a plate of nuts, oranges, and dates for Ahmed to eat. His eyes widened at the sight of this delicious platter. "Ahmed, I want you to take this." He gave the boy several bags of food and opened his closed palm, which held several bills and coins.

"Mr. Massoud, I can't take this. You've been so generous to me already," said Ahmed sheepishly, not wanting to look into the man's eyes. Pushing his hand back, Mr. Massoud explained that Ahmed would be insulting him by not taking the money.

"Ahmed, please come back to my home tonight. You can stay with me and my family, and I will let everyone in the market know

صداقة ידידות صداقة ידידות صداقة ידידות صداقة ידידות

صداقة يديدות صداقة يديدות صداقة يديدות صداقة يديدות

this. If your parents are looking for you, one of the merchants can tell them you're with me, okay?"

"You are the kindest man but I can't. I must find my family." Ahmed knew he was on his way to Netanya, and he wasn't going to say anything to the older man. If it didn't work out there, he would always have a place to stay in Tulkarm.

"I am very satisfied now, Mr. Massoud, so I think I will take a walk and consider my problem. See you later."

"May Allah be with you, Ahmed."

Netanya was only ten miles away—not far really. *I have enough food to allow me to make the trip. My only problem may be at the checkpoint. I'll think about that when I get closer to it.*

As these thoughts ran through his mind, Ahmed was frantically running from one merchant to another in the marketplace. "Have you seen my parents, my sister, my grandfather? Please, my house was demolished and there's nothing left. Someone must have seen them! Someone must know something!"

Mr. Rami grabbed him by the shoulders to calm him down. "Ahmed, we're not sure what happened, except to say that your father resisted the soldiers and was taken away along with your Ommy. I don't know where your sister and grandfather are, or if they went along with your parents. My opinion is that the soldiers wanted to question each member before they would release them.

"The talk is that your father's resistance and anger set off a great suspicion among the soldiers. Please be a guest in my family's home tonight, Ahmed, or for as many nights as it takes until your family returns to find you. And they will, you can be sure of that."

"Thank you, Mr. Rami, but no, I have to find my family. I

صداقة يديدות صداقة يديدות صداقة يديدות صداقة يديدות

صداقة يديدות صداقة يديدות صداقة يديدות صداقة يديدות

cannot sleep or eat until I find them. I must be going now. Pray for me, please."

"Ahmed, wait," called Mr. Rami. "Here are some grapes and oranges, and some nuts to take with you. Be safe." Mr. Rami's eyes began to swell with tears. He suddenly felt old and helpless as he watched the boy take the food from his hands.

"Don't worry, Mr. Rami. I will stay safe, just pray for me." Ahmed's words tried to console him. *Wow, now I have more than enough food for my trip to Netanya. Allahu Akbar.*

Hurriedly, he ran to an area of the marketplace that was vacant and checked his pockets for his identification card for checkpoint passing. Fumbling, he found some coins and a piece of hard ginger candy. *Where is it? I always keep it with me. No, I didn't leave it at the house. I stow my identification card into my pocket each morning.* As he continued to search his pockets, he felt something familiar. *Good, here it is. I knew I had it with me.*

Crumpled and worn from use, he held the card in his hand tightly for fear of losing it. "Next stop, Netanya," Ahmed whispered to himself. "I must locate the Israeli friend of my Abi. He will know how to help me get my family back to Tulkarm." His thoughts were racing as fast as his body was moving, feeling an imposed deadline to reach this Israeli carpet merchant.

Wait, I shouldn't try to get to Netanya now, it's getting too late and the soldiers will be suspicious of me traveling in the evening. Ahmed realized his emotions were confusing his thinking. *I will wait until morning, have some of the fruit Mr. Rami gave me, and then come up with a reason for traveling by myself to Netanya.*

Ahmed searched for an isolated spot in the marketplace to

صداقة يديدות صداقة يديدות صداقة يديدות صداقة يديدות

صداقة يديدوت صداقة يديدوت صداقة يديدوت صداقة يديدوت

rest for the night. Straight ahead he saw the perfect place. As he approached it, he spread his feet around to smooth out the bumps in the dirt so he could have a sleep without pebbles and stones piercing into his body. Ahmed realized it was time for prayers after sunset. Carefully setting himself down on the smoothed dirt, he began his prayers. He looked up at the sky, yearning to be in his bed in a house he once called home.

After completing his prayers, he stretched his body out on the soil and drifted off into a pleasant dream in which Mr. Rami was racing toward him, followed by his parents, grandfather, and sister. "See, Ahmed, I told you everything would be all right. It was a mere technicality; the soldiers just wanted to question the residents of that area of Tulkarm before the houses were razed."

Mr. Rami's smile was so abnormally wide that it mimicked a horror movie villain approaching with the intention to begin gleeful troublemaking. "No!" shouted Ahmed. He jumped up, awaking from sleep and realizing it was just a dream. Shaking his head and yawning, he could feel his weak and tired body lower itself to the ground once again, hoping for a night of sleep.

Then, Ahmed creased his eyes and moved his arm in front of them, trying to shield the hot sun. He thought, *It can't be morning yet. I just fell asleep.* But as he looked around, he could hear the rustling of carts and merchants beginning to set up for the day. He brushed himself off, ran his fingers through his hair, and checked to see how much fruit and nuts he had left.

I'll stop by Mr. Rami and see if he's set up yet. Maybe I can get something to drink from him for my trip. "Oh! I must say my prayers

صداقة يديدوت صداقة يديدوت صداقة يديدوت صداقة يديدوت

صداقة يدِيدות صداقة يدِيدות صداقة يدِيدות صداقة يدِيدות

before I do anything else, or I'll forget as I did yesterday, forgive me, Allah."

After his morning prayers, Ahmed tried to think of a story that would be believable to the soldiers. "What if they keep questioning me? Well, I'll just run as fast as I can, that's what I'll do. ... No, no, what are you thinking, Ahmed? They'll shoot you and then where will you be? You'll be of no use to anyone, wounded or worse, dead."

Trudging toward Mr. Rami's stall, Ahmed whistled and called out, "Aslamalakim, Mr. Rami!"

"Ahmed, my goodness, I thought you had started your search to find your family. What happened?"

"Mr. Rami, it was best for me to sleep and start out this morning; I had to store my energy for my search. Thank you again for the fruit and nuts, but do you have a beverage I can bring with me?" Ahmed squinted as the sun's intensity aimed for him head on.

"Of course, let me see what I have." Mr. Rami hastily searched in the many bottles of juice and came up with a cool bottle of pomegranate juice. "Hah, look what I have for you, special juice to keep you on your feet until you arrive at your destination. Here are several bags of nuts, some oranges and grapes."

"Mr. Rami, you are so kind and generous. My family and I are in deep gratitude to you. Thanking you is not enough, but I do thank you again and again." Ahmed was so humbled by the generosity of Mr. Rami that he knew this was a good omen as he set out on his journey.

صداقة يدِيدות صداقة يدِيدות صداقة يدِيدות صداقة يدِيدות

Chapter 4

As Ahmed walked briskly, he decided to make a game of guessing how far he had walked toward the checkpoint at Netanya. *Every 900 steps I count will be a quarter of a mile, that way I can estimate the miles until I get there. Counting will keep my mind busy as I walk. When I arrive in Netanya, the first thing I will do is go and sit at the shopping mall. That will give me time to rest and think about my next move.*

He behaved as though he had been to Netanya many times. Ahmed had no idea where the mall was or any other place in Netanya; he only remembered the stories he had overheard at the marketplace. He whistled and concentrated on counting each footstep he took.

"There they are," Ahmed said to himself as he observed the soldiers checking people's paperwork in the distance. He also saw many people being turned away. Ahmed felt very nervous and had to come up with a convincing reason why he was going to Netanya. Just then, he heard footsteps and talking behind him. He turned to see two men carrying sacks on their backs.

Ahmed ran to them like they were long-lost relatives. He had an idea. "Asalamalakim. May I please ask a favor of you? I am heading to Netanya, and if I could be a member of your party, I may be able to get through the checkpoint easier. Can I be your

صداقة يديدوت صداقة يديدوت صداقة يديدوت صداقة يديدوت

nephew or grandson or both? Please, it would mean so much to me." His eyes had a pleading look and were lowered out of respect to the elder gentlemen.

One of the men, whose thick, black brows were furrowed with a smirk across his forehead, looked at Ahmed sternly. "Why are you traveling alone in the first place, young man? Where are your elders? It is not safe for you to be by yourself. Don't you realize homes have been bulldozed, and the soldiers are everywhere?"

"Yes, yes, that is why I need to be part of your traveling party. My home was bulldozed, and my parents, sister, and grandfather, are missing. There is nothing left. I was told they were taken away by the soldiers. My Abi has a friend in Netanya who may be able to get information for me. Please, please may I travel with you?" Ahmed's eyes were filled with tears and urgency.

"Well, what do you think?" the elder said to his companion. "Should we take this young man on with us?"

Hesitatingly, his companion rolled his eyes, took a deep breath, exhaled, and said, "I don't think he'll give us any trouble. We'll say he's your grandson, but only if they ask."

"Young man, you are now officially part of our traveling company. What is your name?" Ahmed tried to hold back his excitement. He knew he would now have a better chance of getting to Netanya.

"Thank you, both of you. I will never forget what you are doing for me. My name is Ahmed Quessem," Ahmed said as he extended his hand. "And you are?"

"I am Mr. Mafouz, and this is Mr. Aziz." The pleasantries exchanged, Mr. Mafouz hurried Ahmed along with them as

صداقة يدود صداقة يدود صداقة يدود صداقة يدود

they were getting closer to the checkpoint. Though he felt more confident, he was still anxious. Until he set foot on Netanya's soil, he was not going to take any chances and spoil his plan.

As they walked, Mr. Mafouz asked Ahmed if he had his identification card for the bus to Netanya. *How silly of me*, Ahmed thought, *there is a bus to Netanya.*

"Ahmed, Ahmed, do you have your card? This is no time to be daydreaming," Mr. Mafouz scolded.

"Oh, of course, it is in my traveling bag; see Mr. Mafouz, here it is."

"Good, because we don't want any extra questions asked of us. Have it ready to show the soldier."

"I understand, and I will be more alert." Ahmed peered downward, embarrassed by his boyishness and lack of organization.

As they continued walking, Ahmed could see hands waving about in the distance. He began to feel a flittering in his stomach and wondered if the people at the checkpoint were being given a hard time. He ran to catch up to Mr. Mafouz and Mr. Aziz. "What is going on up ahead?"

"Probably the guards need to see more identification, or they are telling people they can't be allowed to travel into Netanya. So the usual banter is taking place—no need to worry. Just have your card ready and be polite and respectful. Don't give anyone a difficult time, or you'll be turned away, and so will we, grandson/nephew. Ha!" Their pace picked up as they got closer and closer to the checkpoint. Ahmed was becoming more anxious, but he was ready.

They found themselves third in line, and they could see the bus waiting alongside the road. It looked almost full, and Ahmed was

صداقة يديدות صداقة يديدin صداقة يديدות صداقة يديدות

praying that there would be enough room by the time they were checked. *I just can't wait anymore; I have got to get on that bus.*

"Your card, now!" shouted the soldier.

He handed his card over as quickly as he could. "Here it is." *Maybe my politeness will make a good impression.* Ahmed began to panic inside, for it seemed like an eternity.

"Who are you traveling with? These gentlemen?"

"Yes sir, my jiddo and uncle."

"Which one of you is his grandfather?" There was silence. "Come on, come on, we have no time here, but you will have all the time, ha!"

Mr. Mafouz spoke up. "I am his grandfather."

The soldier looked at the identification card. "Your last name is different."

"Yes, this is my daughter's son." Ahmed noticed that Mr. Mafouz and his traveling companion were trying not to appear nervous, but he knew they were.

"Of course, very well." The soldier handed Ahmed's and Mr. Mafouz's cards back to them. "Go on—the bus is almost ready to leave." Those words actually sounded sweet to Ahmed. The soldier continued processing the long line of travelers.

They walked quickly to board the bus. As they walked, Ahmed whispered to Mr. Mafouz, "That was a close one. I didn't think we would make it."

"Sshh. Don't say anything. Just walk and get on the bus." The three of them stepped up into the bus. Mr. Mafouz noticed two seats in the back and one midway in.

صداقة يديدות صداقة يديدות صداقة يديدות صداقة يديدות

صداقة ידידות صداقة ידידות صداقة ידידות صداقة ידידות

"You sit over here," Mr. Mafouz said and pointed to the seat for Ahmed. "We will sit in the back."

This was a strange duo, Ahmed thought to himself. *Mr. Mafouz seems to be the one in charge, and Mr. Aziz just follows along.*

The bus ride was not as long as he expected even with several stops, and as they got closer, Ahmed was more excited for he had never been to Netanya. His Abi used to tell him stories about the great city by the sea and the trips to the carpet merchant for the family's prayer rugs. Ahmed couldn't remember the merchant's name, but he knew he was Israeli. Ahmed's Abi spoke highly of the Israeli who had befriended him, and he had looked forward to his visits to the man and his son when he was a young boy. After the recent attack at the mall, visits by Tulkarm merchants to Netanya were extremely limited.

Ahmed wondered if he could locate this carpet merchant and see if the man would help him try to locate his family. He believed his family had been taken out of Tulkarm to another area, but he didn't know where. Ahmed was certain of one thing: he would not rest until he knew his family's whereabouts. His thoughts began to cause drowsiness as he closed his eyes to take the first rest he had since starting out this morning.

صداقة ידידות صداقة ידידות صداقة ידידות صداقة ידידות

Chapter 5

"Wake up, Ahmed." He felt a push into his shoulder and then a pull on his arm. As he awakened, he looked up to see Mr. Mafouz walking down to the exit of the bus.

Am I really here? Ahmed made sure he had his card and bag, than he walked down the aisle and exited the bus. "Well, Mr. Mafouz and Mr. Aziz, thank you again for helping me get to Netanya."

"Where are you going? You shouldn't be wandering around by yourself. You could be picked up by soldiers or security and find yourself in the same predicament as your family."

"I'll be okay after I find my Abi's friend—a carpet merchant in Netanya."

Puzzled and amused, Mr. Mafouz laughed. "Ahmed, do you think there is only one carpet merchant in Netanya? Actually, I don't know that there are any left. They have closed down because the larger department stores are selling carpets. You are going to be one busy fellow, but good luck to you."

As he turned to go, he added, "Listen, Ahmed, we will be at the checkpoint for the return to Tulkarm at four o'clock. If you change your mind, meet us there."

"Thank you. I will consider it. Have a good day to both of you,

صداقة ידידות صداقة ידידות صداقة ידידות صداقة ידידות

good-bye." Mr. Mafouz had a strange feeling he would never see Ahmed again and wished him well.

Ahmed looked around, puzzled, and then decided to ask someone how to get to Yaffa Ben Ami Garden. He didn't know what to look at first; there was so much to see. His stomach began to quiver from the excitement of everything around him, but he also realized he was very hungry. Ahmed pulled some dried fruit and juice from his bag.

"Hmm … just what my poor body needed." He gulped the juice quickly, not realizing how warm it had gotten. "Ugh. I'll wait until I can buy something cold." Ahmed grimaced and put the bottle away.

He walked a short while longer, not looking directly at anyone he passed. He could feel people staring at him suspiciously as he walked, and he hoped he wouldn't be stopped. Cars began to speed by; buses, taxis, and people came from every direction. *This city is very different from the marketplace and Tulkarm,* Ahmed thought. Up ahead he thought he saw the gardens. He looked at the signs, which read "Petah" and "Hertsel" and realized he had made it to the gardens.

Ahmed found a bench and settled down. The food packages he saw people buying from the vendors made him hungry. *I must have some change to buy something, anything. Please, please find some change.* Ahmed frantically emptied his bag and reached into his pants pockets. He pulled out some coins and bills that Mr. Mafouz had given him, and he approached the vendor to see what he could buy.

"May I have a falafel sandwich please?"

"Anything to drink, young man?" the vendor asked.

صداقة ידידות صداقة ידידות صداقة ידידות صداقة ידידות

صداقة يديدوت صداقة يديدوت صداقة يديدوت صداقة يديدوت

"I don't think I have enough," he said softly. Ahmed's eyes looked down and away from the vendor.

"You're not from Netanya, are you?" Ahmed didn't answer and kept his head looking downward. "Well, here's your sandwich, and we have a special today. The drink comes with the sandwich, enjoy."

Slowly raising his eyes, with a faint smile on his face, Ahmed took his lunch, and though it could barely be heard, said, "Thank you." The vendor smiled and stared at Ahmed as he disappeared down the street.

Ahmed walked quickly back to the bench. He tore open his sandwich and drink. As he bit into the sandwich, he could barely taste the food that was finding its way to his hungry stomach. He continued to enjoy his well-deserved lunch, when he saw a boy about his age staring at him. Ahmed stared back, his eyes squinting at the figure coming his way. He didn't want anyone figuring out that he wasn't from Netanya. The food vendor was quick to point it out. That would mean big trouble for him. Ahmed felt lucky that the vendor didn't continue with his questioning, but he wasn't sure if his luck would hold out.

He started to put his food into his bag and got up to walk away when he saw the boy smiling at him. "Shalom. Do you mind if I sit down?" he asked.

Ahmed turned away and said, "This is a public bench, of course you can."

"Where are you from? You're not from here are you?" Ahmed didn't answer. "Where are you from? I know it's not Netanya."

"What gives you that idea? It doesn't matter, anyway. It won't make a difference in your life, now will it?" Ahmed stared at him.

صداقة يديدوت صداقة يديدوت صداقة يديدوت صداقة يديدوت

صداقة ידידות صداقة ידידות صداقة ידידות صداقة ידידות

He started to turn to walk away, but there was an uncomfortable moment of silence as he and the other boy eyed one another. Ahmed wanted to get away as fast as he could, but this boy's stare almost created a spell over his feet. He couldn't move.

The boy spoke again. "I'm sorry to assume you're not from here, but you're carrying a bag, and excuse me, but your shorts and T-shirt look like you've been rolling in dirt, and your accent is not Israeli, so I—"

"Maybe I should ask you who you are. You seem very comfortable annoying people you don't know."

"Sorry, I shouldn't think that you would graciously accept my friendly gesture, especially an outsider like you," he replied sarcastically. "Would you like to hear about me? No? Well, I'm going to tell you anyway."

A slight smirk appeared on Ahmed's face. He sat down on the bench. "I guess I don't have a chance escaping you, do I?"

"No, you don't, alien. My name is Joshua Atai, I'm fifteen, and I have lived here in Netanya all my life. Perhaps that is the reason for my comfort—the familiarity of my city and its people. My Aba has a carpet store with beautiful carpets and prayer rugs. Anything you want, my Aba has or can get for you. … That is, he used to be able to get it for his customers. Unfortunately he will be closing at the end of August.

"My Ima is an artist who owns an art gallery near the beach and shows art locally from all over the world. She has several artists from the United States showing right now. I have a younger sister, Ashira, who can be really irritating at times, but since I'm the older brother, she knows I can help her, so I'm in control, ha! Thank

صداقة ידידות صداقة ידידות صداقة ידידות صداقة ידידות

صداقة يدّيدوت صداقة يديدوت صداقة يديدوت صداقة يديدوت

goodness she is away at camp for the summer. Me, I love soccer and must say I'm pretty good at it; I'm on the local soccer team. Well, that's it. Now it's your turn. Start with your name."

Hesitatingly, Ahmed was trying to evaluate the situation and this boy sitting next to him. He was very friendly and a little strange but maybe he could help him. "Look, I don't know you, but you seem to be friendly enough, but then again, why should I trust you?"

"Probably because there's no one else around, and you would be picked up in a heartbeat. What? You think you're so special that security won't know you're an outsider?" Joshua was rapidly firing off reasons, when Ahmed interrupted.

"Please try to understand my situation before you jump to any conclusions. I am not a troublemaker and not looking to cause any problems. I have enough of my own right now. My name is Ahmed Quessem, and I'm also fifteen—and you're right, I'm not from Netanya. I am a Palestinian born and raised in Tulkarm. My parents' home was destroyed because of its close location to the security wall. It was demolished yesterday.

"I was on an errand for my Ommy and when I returned, our home was gone, and I couldn't find them. None of the people I knew could tell me anything except that my Abi had been arguing with the soldiers, and they took him and my Ommy away. I'm desperate to find them. Because my Abi had a childhood Israeli friend from Netanya where my jiddo bought prayer rugs, I thought he might help me locate my family. So, with the kindness of two gentlemen, I accompanied them on the bus and arrived a short

صداقة يدّيدوت صداقة يديدوت صداقة يديدوت صداقة يديدوت

صداقة يدّيدوت صداقة يدّيدوت صداقة يدّيدوت صداقة يدّيدوت

while ago. That's my story. … Didn't you say your father has a carpet store? Where is it located, and how long has he been there?"

Joshua was confused. "My father's store has little inventory; most of the rugs have been sold. He doesn't even go in anymore, maybe once a week just to be sure everything is safe." Joshua extended his hand in a friendly gesture. Ahmed followed with his hand, and they both shook and smiled at each other.

"I just thought that perhaps," Ahmed interrupted, "you might know the man's name. How long has it been since your Abi spoke to this man or did business with him? Really, you thought you would make a trip to Netanya and find this person who your Abi hasn't seen in what, twenty or thirty years? You must be kidding."

"I don't know anything; just that my Abi always said if people could get along as well as he and this man, the Israelis and Palestinians would know peace. So I am here in Netanya to try and find him, and I am hoping that he can help me locate my parents. I know I'm taking a great risk being here by myself, but I don't care. I must find my parents. They did nothing wrong, and I'm not going to let them rot in an Israeli security cell. My parents are not criminals. I hope you don't think that taking someone's house away and destroying it is all right."

"Sorry. You don't need to be so defensive."

"I'm tired and still hungry, and I want to be home with my parents. You think I want to be sitting here in a strange place not knowing anyone? Well, except you. Everything is messed up. People's homes shouldn't be destroyed. My family did nothing to deserve this."

"Calm down, Ahmed. It's an ugly situation for sure. Listen,

صداقة يديدوت صداقة يديدوت صداقة يديدوت صداقة يديدوت

I'll try to help you but don't speak loudly when we walk away from here, got it?"

"Yeah, okay. I was just thinking, wouldn't it be very strange if your father turned out to be the man I am looking for?"

"It would be, but I doubt that. Wow! That's quite a story, Ahmed. Listen, why don't you come to my home for dinner tonight? I'll call my parents and tell them I'm bringing home a guest. What do you say?"

Ahmed didn't answer right away. He just didn't believe that this could have been so easy, but he was nervous too. *If this man isn't my Abi's friend, he could throw me out of his house, or worse, call the authorities to come and get me. Then what?*

"Well, Ahmed, what do you say? It could be fun, and you may just get lucky and find the person who can help you."

"Joshua, you're going to ask your parents if you could bring home some Palestinian vagrant who's wandering around Netanya looking for his parents who may be in an Israeli prison? Are you crazy?"

"My parents are understanding people. They don't jump to conclusions at the start. My Aba analyzes everything and then makes a decision."

Ahmed considered Joshua's words. The other boy seemed sincere, and he wouldn't waste his time talking to him or would he? He did offer the invitation, and Ahmed was desperate for food. *By this evening, who knows where I could get any food, or even if I would have a place to lay my head down?*

"Will you?" said Joshua. "I promise I'm not going to do anything to get you in trouble. I understand your situation, but

صداقة يدידות صداقة يدידות صداقة يدידות صداقة يدידות

you know what a risk you have taken being here by yourself? It's one thing to come with your parent to do business; however, if security suspects anything, they'll bring you in without question. You, my new vagrant friend, are more secure with me."

"Okay, I guess so. I accept your invitation, but I have to ask you, why would you invite a total stranger to your home, especially an outsider and a Palestinian?"

Laughing, Joshua knew why this might seem strange, but offered this explanation. "Ahmed, you're a good person, I can see that, and I like you. I think we may have a lot in common, don't you? Oh, and you looked lonely and pathetic sitting on this bench, and definitely in need of a bath. What else could I do?"

They both laughed so hard, pulling each other's arms and rocking back and forth. Joshua chuckled and patted Ahmed on the back.

"Joshua, this is my first time in Netanya. My Abi told me many stories about this beautiful city. I have never traveled outside of Tulkarm before, and I would really love to see the beach here. Do you think you could take me to see it, please?"

"Of course I could, but I thought you were anxious to find out about your parents." Joshua seemed puzzled.

"Yes, yes, I desperately want to find my family, but since it's not happening tonight, I have an urge to see this beach that is supposed to be so beautiful. I will never have an opportunity like this again. Can you understand, Joshua? Do you think I am being selfish?"

"No, you are just naturally curious." Joshua's eyes sparkled, and his mouth opened wide. Ahmed knew from his new friend's smile that he would see the first beach of his entire lifetime. Joshua

صداقة يدידות صداقة يدידות صداقة يدידות صداقة يدידות

صداقة يديدوت صداقة يديدوت صداقة يديدوت صداقة يديدوت

pulled out his cell phone and called his parents. Ima, his mother, answered.

"Ima, I would like to bring a friend home for dinner tonight. Do you think that is possible? Do you have to go back to the gallery this evening?"

"Actually, Arella will be keeping the gallery open this evening. Who is this friend? Noah, Jonah?"

"No, Ima, it is a new friend I met today at Yaffa Gardens. His name is Ahmed. You will meet him tonight. Please say yes, Ima, please?"

"Ahmed? He is not an Israeli boy?"

"Ima, please just say yes, and I know you will meet and like him; he's a lot like me. I'll tell you all about him. Actually, he'll tell you himself." Joshua let out nervous laughter.

Ahmed couldn't quite translate the communication as Joshua's animated face kept changing from smiles to frowns to elation. There was a moment of silence, and Joshua's face froze in time. Then he began to move around in a circle with the phone to his ear, his head bobbing up and down as he waited for his mother's answer.

"All right, Joshua, you may bring your friend, Ahmed, but sometime after dinner we will need to talk about this boy and what he's doing in Netanya by himself. Be careful and don't bring attention to yourselves. Don't speak to one another unless you do it very quietly, and if you see security, say nothing. If you are approached, *you*, not Ahmed, answers any questions, understand?"

"Yes, and thank you so much, Ima. You will like him. I'm taking him to Sironit Beach. We're going to use the elevator so he can get a good view of the sea."

صداقة يديدوت صداقة يديدوت صداقة يديدوت صداقة يديدوت

صداقة يديدوت صداقة يديدوت صداقة يديدوت صداقة يديدوت

"Okay, Joshua, just be careful. Dinner will be at six o'clock. Be on time," was his mother's authoritative command.

As Joshua put his phone away, he grabbed Ahmed by the shoulders. "Let's go, friend, for your first visit to the amazing beaches of Netanya. We'll go up Hertsel Street and walk to the promenade on the beach. Are you excited?"

Ahmed was thinking how strange it was that fate would shine upon him in the form of an Israeli boy. Ahmed's teeth glistened in the sun, and they seemed to reflect happiness. For the first time since he left Tulkarm, Ahmed felt confident about finding his parents. He gently touched Joshua's back and said, "Thank you."

"Let's see who can run the fastest down Hertsel Street!" Joshua chanted loudly. After several blocks, Ahmed slowed down with Joshua following.

"Let's just finish walking there, my friend." Ahmed took a few deep breaths in and out to get himself in control again. They continued walking, and Ahmed began to see the sky open up become more vast. "This is amazing, Joshua. … Do you have anything to snack on?" Ahmed began to rub his stomach.

Joshua handed Ahmed a piece of brightly wrapped candy. "Calm down, Ahmed; it's just the sea. Relax and enjoy it; we're almost there."

Ahmed didn't seem to be listening and began to quickly rip open the candy and put it into his mouth. Their pace quickened as they began their walk to the promenade and to the sea. There were people everywhere, smiling, seemingly happy. He thought back to his town and the people in it. They all appeared serious, rarely smiling. But he also remembered that they didn't have a beautiful

صداقة يديدوت صداقة يديدوت صداقة يديدوت صداقة يديدوت

صداقة ידידות صداقة ידידות صداقة ידידות صداقة ידידות

sea to look at, and they were worried about the wall that was being erected. Then he thought about the people here who worried about suicide bombings. *Is there any real happiness and safety for anyone?* he wondered.

As they approached the promenade, Joshua noticed Ahmed's watery eyes. He didn't say anything and let his friend enjoy the view. He motioned to Ahmed to continue their walk. Turning to Joshua, Ahmed asked him, "How can the world be as beautiful as this and yet has people in it who are so cruel and filled with hate?"

"Wow, Ahmed, I thought this would make you happy, not so depressingly philosophical." Joshua knew all too well what he was feeling, because he felt the same way. He had never put it in the same terms as Ahmed had just done.

The warm breeze felt good on Ahmed's face. He raised his head so the sun would warm his face and neck. Ahmed smiled as the heat created trickles of perspiration down his cheeks. Lifting his hand to wipe his face, he turned to Joshua. "Life is truly good for you here—the sun, sand, and beach give a person what they need—a panoramic vision of their spirituality."

"Hmmm …" Joshua began to open his mouth to speak, looked toward the sea, and remained silent. "Maybe tomorrow I'll take you to the mall, what do you say, Ahmed? Would you like that?"

"I don't know if I will be here tomorrow. I may head back to Tulkarm after dinner if there is a bus available, or maybe I'll just walk."

"Are you crazy? No, no absolutely not. You would be stopped at the checkpoint, if you even got that far. A young Palestinian boy traveling alone in Netanya, are you kidding? They would spot you

صداقة ידידות صداقة ידידות صداقة ידידות صداقة ידידות

in a second. They're very shrewd and quick. Then they would ask you lots of questions, and who knows where you would be. You will stay at my house tonight, get a good meal, and rest. After you speak to my Aba, tomorrow I will help you find this rug merchant friend of your Abi's, okay?"

The sound of waves in the distance gave Ahmed some peace. Taking a deep breath, he said, "Okay. You have a good plan. Patience is everything, isn't it, Joshua?"

Joshua nodded and began walking from the promenade back down toward Hertsel. Ahmed followed his lead and turned to look back at the sea one last time. "We're going home now. You'll meet my parents—my sister is away at camp—and you'll have a delicious meal. My Ima is a fantastic cook." Joshua offered this information to Ahmed without hesitation.

As they walked down Hertsel, the buildings began to recede and the street started to look like a family neighborhood. Some houses were small, while others were grand; some had front gardens filled with flowers. The street was immaculate and so were the houses. Ahead was a two-story, white building that was partially hidden behind a concrete wall.

"Come on, Ahmed." Joshua began running toward the white building, and Ahmed followed. Joshua opened the gate to a large front yard filled with flowers, pots, and overgrown bushes. There were chairs nestled behind a bush filled with beautiful white flowers. Ahmed could see beyond to a courtyard that looked similar to his home—the home he once had. In a corner of the courtyard was a beautiful palm tree. Ahmed thought he saw someone's arm lifting a cup.

صداقة ידידות صداقة ידידות صداقة ידידות صداقة ידידות

صداقة يديدوت صداقة يديدوت صداقة يديدوت صداقة يديدوت

Joshua called out, "Ima, Ahmed and I are here." From where Ahmed has seen the arm, now a woman emerged from the garden chair.

"Shalom, hello, you must be Ahmed. I am Joshua's Ima, Mrs. Atai." Ahmed did not look directly into her eyes and whispered some words that were barely audible. Mrs. Atai excused herself and told Joshua dinner would be ready shortly.

"Ahmed, you don't have to be afraid. Ima welcomed you here. Let's go to my room, or do you want to play some ball?"

"Ball for sure. Let's kick a few balls and practice our championship soccer skills."

"Great, let's go," said Joshua as he hurried off to find a ball.

The yard had a profusion of flowers in colors that Ahmed had never seen before. He found comfort in looking at them for they made him feel like he was home. While he was studying the flowers, Joshua kicked the ball and took him by surprise. Ahmed quickly moved his legs and returned the ball to Joshua. The ball kept up a steady pace as each one ran to kick it back to the other.

"Joshua," Ima called, "Come in for dinner."

Ahmed slowed the ball down and threw it to Joshua. "You're really good, Joshua. I wish our teams could play together."

"That would be great, but a dream," Joshua said as they approached the courtyard door leading into the kitchen. "Maybe someday, Ahmed," he added.

They walked through the kitchen past Mrs. Atai. Ahmed followed Joshua into a long hallway to the door of the bathroom. This home was unlike anything Ahmed had ever seen. Everything was modern, and his Ima's kitchen had all the latest appliances

صداقة يديدوت صداقة يديدوت صداقة يديدوت صداقة يديدوت

صداقة ידידות صداقة ידידות صداقة ידידות صداقة ידידות

with a huge countertop displaying large platters of fruit. His eyes couldn't move quickly enough to take in all that he was trying to see in the doorways to the other rooms.

There was beautiful artwork on the walls and colorful rugs. Ahmed was looking around at everything when he passed a table with an array of family pictures. As he walked by, one picture in particular caught his eye. It was a picture of Joshua, his mother and father, his sister, and he imagined an older brother. But Joshua had never mentioned an older brother, and Ahmed felt uncomfortable asking.

The smells of the kitchen had Ahmed anxious to sit down for dinner. "Ahmed, why don't you wash up in this bathroom, and I'll do the same after you."

"Sure." Ahmed couldn't believe the size of the bathroom. He looked at himself in the mirror as he washed his hands to get ready for dinner. He came out of the bathroom and announced, "I'm done, Joshua. Your turn."

A few minutes later, Joshua walked in while Ahmed stood there looking at the corner of the room. "Let's go, Ahmed."

Ahmed followed Joshua back down the hallway and into the kitchen. It was a large, bright, sun-filled room that had more beautiful artwork. The table was set with unusual tableware that looked handmade. Sitting at the table was a dark-haired man who stared intently as Ahmed came over to the table.

"Aba, this is Ahmed. Ahmed, this is my Aba, Mr. Atai."

"I am pleased to meet you, sir, and thank you for sharing your dinner table with me tonight."

"Shalom, Ahmed. Welcome and please have a seat." Joshua's

صداقة ידידות صداقة ידידות صداقة ידידות صداقة ידידות

صداقة ידידות صداقة ידידות صداقة ידידות صداقة ידידות

father seemed friendly enough, but there was sadness in his eyes. Ahmed sat down next to him and noticed a large picture on the wall with a handsome young man who looked to be about twenty years old.

"Where are you from, and what brings you here alone?" Joshua's father asked.

"I'm from Tulkarm, and I'm here to find a friend of my Abi who is a carpet merchant."

"Ah, Tulkarm, the West Bank. There was a time when travel to Netanya was not strictly limited as it is now. Even now, when the soldiers are in a bad mood, they turn people away."

Ahmed didn't look Joshua's Aba directly in the eyes for he feared that he would be asked questions he did not want to answer. Instead, he focused on the smell of a delicious roast chicken that was set on the table. The chicken glistened, and the aroma of fresh lemons made its way to Ahmed's nose. Following the chicken were artichokes, whose fragrance reminded him of his mother's kitchen.

"Hmmm …" Ahmed swooned. A platter of Israeli couscous filled with carrots, eggplant, and dried fruits found a place next to the chicken. Ahmed whispered to Joshua, "You were right. Your Ima is a wonderful cook like my Ommy, Joshua."

"Don't be shy, Ahmed. You can tell Ima what you told me." Ahmed's face turned a deep red like a burst cherry, and Joshua realized how he embarrassed Ahmed.

"Ima, Ahmed is very impressed with your cooking. He wanted you to know that."

"Thank you, Ahmed."

Joshua's father took a piece of matzo and brought the glass

صداقة ידידות صداقة ידידות صداقة ידידות صداقة ידידות

صداقة يدي دوت صداقة يدي دوت صداقة يدي دوت صداقة يدي دوت

of wine closer to him. "We will now say our Shabbat prayers. Ahmed, you may say your prayers silently if you wish." As Joshua's Aba began reciting the prayers for Shabbat, Ahmed couldn't help thinking how so many traditions in Joshua's household were similar to his own. For the first time since the disappearance of his family, Ahmed felt at peace.

"Amen," sounded the end of the prayers, and Ima proclaimed, "Everyone enjoy."

The plates were passed until everyone had enough of what they wanted. Out of respect, Ahmed waited until Joshua's parents ate their first forkful and then began his meal. When he looked up, he realized his plate was clean, while everyone was still savoring each mouthful. Ahmed looked at his plate and began to feel self-conscious.

When Mrs. Atai noticed Ahmed's discomfort, she said, "Here, Ahmed." She passed the plate of chicken and encouraged him by saying, "Please have another helping. Have some artichokes too—whatever you would like."

"Thank you, Mrs. Atai. Your cooking is hard to resist." She and Ahmed exchanged smiles. Staring at Ahmed, Aba asked him why he made the trip to Netanya to find his Abi's friend. He said that seemed like an ambitious journey to take on his own, as well as risky for him as a young Palestinian boy.

Ahmed began to explain. "As you probably know, the Israeli soldiers have begun building a security wall between Tulkarm and Netanya. My family and others were told that they had to take all their belongings and leave within a certain time. Yesterday, my Ommy had asked me to do an errand, and when I returned home,

صداقة يدي دوت صداقة يدي دوت صداقة يدي دوت صداقة يدي دوت

صداقة يديدوت صداقة يديدوت صداقة يديدوت صداقة يديدوت

our house was gone, knocked down until there was nothing left but the rubble of the concrete and dirt.

"When I tried to look for anything that was left behind, the soldiers came closer and ordered me to leave. I couldn't find my family and asked the merchants at the market, but they couldn't tell me anything. My father's friend in Netanya knew a lot of people, so I thought he might be able to help me to locate them. I thought they may have been taken out of Tulkarm to a security station.

"Allah was with me the day I planned to get on the bus to Netanya. I met two gentlemen who allowed me to travel with them. One of them told the checkpoint officer that I was his grandson so there wouldn't be suspicion about my presence. I was lucky enough to meet Joshua, though I wasn't sure if I could trust him. He convinced me that he was honest and wasn't trying to get me into trouble, and here I am, enjoying your kind hospitality."

"That's quite a story, Ahmed, and for someone so young. You are a very strong-willed and independent boy." Aba seemed impressed. "Do you know this merchant's name?"

"No, I don't, but my Abi used to tell me stories about him, what a kind man he was and how his Aba always spent time talking to him about everything. My Abi had a lot of respect for him, and he and my jiddo would visit frequently to purchase prayer rugs. This man's son became a friend of my Abi. He said he had the best quality rugs, much better than the ones my jiddo would see in the markets in Tulkarm. My Abi would say if there were more people like him, there would be peace in our cities."

"Well, Ahmed, your Abi sounds like a very wise man."

Joshua's Aba got up from his chair and walked over to the

صداقة يديدوت صداقة يديدوت صداقة يديدوت صداقة يديدوت

wall where the picture of the young man hung. He took it off the wall and brought it back to the table. Ahmed could see Joshua's Ima become visibly upset. As she began to get up from her chair, Aba placed his hand on her arm and squeezed it as tears trickled down her cheeks. She walked to the sink, turning her back from everyone.

"Ahmed, I'm going to tell you a story now about this picture and the young man in it." Joshua's face became frozen and serious, unlike the boy Ahmed had met earlier. "This was our son Avram. He was older than Joshua by five years. In this picture, he was twenty and had been enlisted in the Israeli army for two years. This was his duty to his country and his people, and he was very proud to do it. I'm telling you this because I want you to understand how each family can be affected by unnecessary and cruel events and how the cycle of violence continues because of them.

"Avram was well prepared to be a good soldier; he received excellent training. Avram and other soldiers were assigned to the hotel in Netanya during the Passover holiday to keep peace and order so that people could celebrate. It was not meant to be. A suicide bomber detonated a bomb that killed many of the Passover celebrants. Avram and several other soldiers were also killed."

Ahmed's eyes widened, and he began to speak but was stopped by Aba who went on. "We were having our family Passover when we received the news. My consolation, what lessens my grief, is that my son was there to protect families who were celebrating Passover just as his own family was that day."

"I am so-o-o sorry. I ... I don't know what I can say to all of

صداقة يديدوت صداقة يديدوت صداقة يديدوت صداقة يديدوت

you." Ahmed's face was ashen, and his words broke apart as he said them.

"Ahmed, you don't have to say anything. I want to continue, please," Aba said. "Because of the horror of that day, the Israeli government made the decision to limit travel from Tulkarm into Netanya. They thought it would prevent more incidents like the Passover one. After that, the bombing at the mall was the last straw for the Israelis, and another decision was made to begin to erect a wall to keep everyone in Tulkarm on their side and away from us. This wall was to protect the Israelis from others trying to come in from the other cities in the West Bank.

"What I am trying to tell you is that one event causes many more events to happen as a reaction to them. These decisions just pour acid on the open wound. It doesn't make the wound heal; it only makes it fester and become even greater than it was originally. People become angrier and more hostile, and it serves no purpose other than to give people new ways to harm one another."

Aba seemed sad and accepting of what happened to his son, and he made it clear that he believed travel restrictions and walls may cut down on the bombing incidents, but these would not make anything better between the Israelis and Palestinians.

He went on, "I don't hate those who were involved in the bombing incident, because they are a product of the propaganda and ideology put out by hate groups. Those same people from their community will become even angrier now that the wall is being built, and they will find new ways to hurt others. This is what I mean about the cycle continuing. When will it end, if ever?"

Ahmed sat silent and felt that anything he said wouldn't have

صداقة يديدوت صداقة يديدوت صداقة يديدوت صداقة يديدوت

the impact or sincerity he wanted to convey. Joshua interrupted the silence. "Aba, if I may say something. Ahmed and I want to try and find the carpet merchant that his father knew. Do you have any ideas as to where he should start?"

Mrs. Atai came back to the table and began clearing the plates. The Shabbat candles flickered as she walked by, and she seemed to pause when she passed Avram's picture. Mr. Atai cleared his throat and began, "Well, this may not be easy, because you don't even know if this man still exists. He may have moved, died, gone out of business—but let me think this over, and I will let you know later this evening or tomorrow, okay?"

"Thank you, Aba," Joshua responded.

"Thank you, Mr. Atai," Ahmed added.

Mrs. Atai walked toward the table carrying a beautiful cake and set it down. Joshua's and Ahmed's eyes widened to twice the size. They turned to one another and smiled. Mrs. Atai went to get some plates, but Joshua excitedly said, "Ima, I'll get them for you."

Ima knew Joshua couldn't wait another minute to stick his fork into a piece of the homemade apple cake. "Thank you." She chuckled to herself as she knew Joshua's intentions.

Joshua sliced an extra-large piece for his guest. "Here you go, Ahmed. This is the best ever. You will really like this," he told his new friend.

"Thank you. You're right. This is the best ever. Mr. and Mrs. Atai, thank you for the dinner and for making me very welcome in your home," Ahmed acknowledged. He hoped that his good fortune would continue. "Mmmm … Mrs. Atai, you are a good baker."

صداقة يديدوت صداقة يديدوت صداقة يديدوت صداقة يديدوت

صداقة يديدות صداقة يديدות صداقة يديدות صداقة يديدות

"Thank you, Ahmed. Does your Ima bake?"

"Oh yes," said Ahmed enthusiastically. "She makes cakes and pastries with fruits and nuts. My favorite is her fig cake. This reminds me of it," he said sadly.

"I'm sure you will be eating it again very soon," Mrs. Atai responded. She could see the sadness as his eyes lowered and his face drooped.

"Ahmed, as soon as we finish, let's excuse ourselves and go to my room. We'll figure out a plan for tomorrow and then we'll talk to Aba later on."

"That sounds like a good plan, Joshua, but first things first, and that means enjoying this cake."

Everyone laughed at Ahmed's comment, and the room seemed to take on a more joyous atmosphere. Ahmed bowed his head down from embarrassment. He was very shy around strangers, but he felt comfortable and safe in the company of the Atais.

The boys left the table and went to Joshua's room. They sat on the floor and Ahmed began, "You know when your Aba was talking about Avram? I could see how much he missed him and felt some relief in talking about him. I was feeling the same way about my family as I listened to him retell the story. I began to feel that if I spoke about my family, it would be as though I was trying to make them come alive again, just like your Aba was doing with Avram. Do you understand what I'm saying, Joshua?" Ahmed said quizzically.

There was silence for a moment as Joshua stared down at the floor. "Yeah, I do understand too well, but the only difference is that

صداقة يدﯾدوت صداقة يدﯾدوت صداقة يدﯾدوت صداقة يدﯾدوت

your parents are alive and are okay, I just know it. For my brother, it will never be again."

"I'm so sorry. I didn't mean to say …" Ahmed regretted his words.

"It's okay, Ahmed, honest. This is life, and we can't change it. I know what you are trying to say. Forget it—let's play some chess. Do you know how to play?"

"No, but will you teach me? I've always wanted to learn to play, and I'm a fast learner."

"Sure, I'll get the board and chess pieces. We'll see how fast you are when I overtake you." As Joshua set the board up, he explained the various pieces to Ahmed. Ahmed rolled his eyes and sighed deeply. His eyes narrowed and his forehead showed lines that should not appear on a young boy's face.

"Are you okay, Ahmed? You seem confused."

"No, no, go ahead. I just look this way when I'm concentrating." He paused and then asked, "Joshua, do you think about your brother? I mean what happened to him? Do you hate the people who killed him?" He kept his head down, but his eyes rolled upward as he wondered what Joshua's reaction would be.

"If you think I feel the same way as my father, you're wrong!" Joshua's voice raised to a pitch Ahmed had not heard before.

"Forget it, Joshua." Ahmed said anxiously.

"No, I will answer your question. I hated everyone who looked like you and talked like you. I couldn't understand how anyone could do this—to my brother, to the children, parents, and grandparents of the Israeli people. But the more I thought about it and everything that has gone on among our people, I also couldn't

صداقة يدﯾدوت صداقة يدﯾدوت صداقة يدﯾدوت صداقة يدﯾدوت

صداقة ידידות صداقة ידידות صداقة ידידות صداقة ידידות

understand why we would do the same thing to the Palestinians. Nothing gets accomplished, and people just get angrier and more hateful toward each other. We give each other reasons to hate. Then I met you, Ahmed." Joshua's lips turned upward, and a slight smile ran across his face.

"Wow, Joshua, I felt the same way until I met you, although my Abi's close Israeli friend had an appreciation for humanity. My Abi's stories about him showed me a good and kind side. We share so much, but you and I both know that when I return to Tulkarm, things will go on as they always do." Ahmed's voice held a whisper of sadness.

"Let's get a good night's sleep so we can start out early tomorrow. In the morning we'll come up with a plan so we can get to all the carpet dealers and hopefully find the one you want to meet and talk to about your Abi. My Aba might have information to help us. He'll let us know by morning."

Ahmed fixed the makeshift bed, and before he slipped under the covers, he knelt down to say a final prayer before sleep. Joshua stared at Ahmed as he slipped into a state of silence. His eyes fixed on Ahmed's every move. He smiled and nodded his head approvingly.

Ahmed finished his prayers and called out, "Good night, Joshua."

"Good night, Ahmed. Sleep well."

صداقة ידידות صداقة ידידות صداقة ידידות صداقة ידידות

Chapter 6

A flash of orange and yellow passed across Joshua's eyes and startled him into waking. He sat up and looked away from the sunlight that was streaming through the window. As he stared at the clock and then down at Ahmed's bed, he saw the covers pushed aside and an empty spot where he had slept. Joshua felt a surge of panic as he jumped out of bed to look for his friend. He heard some movement, and as he approached the kitchen, he saw Ahmed standing in front of his brother's picture, gazing at it as though in a trance.

Joshua quietly observed Ahmed from a distance. *What is he doing?* he wondered. *And why isn't he moving?* He quietly turned around to go back to his room, then he heard, "Good morning, Joshua. I had the best sleep, did you?"

Joshua wanted to ask Ahmed about the picture, but he wasn't sure he wanted to hear his reason for studying it.

"Good morning, boys," Joshua's mother spoke from the dining room.

"Good morning, Ima. Did Aba go to the store?"

"No, he's out in the garden. Please don't disturb him—you know his morning ritual. He'll be in shortly. I'll make some shakshouka and challah for you before you head out the door this morning. Ahmed, have you said your morning prayers?"

صداقة ידידות صداقة ידידות صداقة ידידות صداقة ידידות

"Yes, I have upon rising this morning. Thank you, Mrs. Atai." Ahmed was taken by surprise at Mrs. Atai's thoughtfulness for reminding him about his prayers.

"Ahmed, let's go to my room and come up with a plan. Ima will call us in when it's ready."

Back in Joshua's room, Ahmed told his friend, "You're really taking this seriously." He watched as Joshua started writing, "The Plan" on his notebook paper. Step one: check out all the carpet merchants in Netanya (that will be easy, there aren't many of them!). Step two: put them in order from the closest to the farthest away from the house. Step three: visit each merchant and match the description of the owner to Ahmed's description. Step four …

"Joshua, I get it, you are an obsessive one, aren't you?" Ahmed laughed. "But I still like you."

Joshua pushed Ahmed, embarrassed about his need for a detailed plan. "Hey, watch out."

They began a friendly wrestle and then Ima called, "Come boys, breakfast is ready!" Joshua got in one last hold as they stood up and took deep breaths so that Ima wouldn't ask questions.

Joshua studied Ahmed with envy as he ate his breakfast with passion. "Why are you smirking, Joshua?" Ahmed gave him a confused look. "Aren't you hungry? Am I much more interesting than breakfast, my friend?" Ahmed's beautiful smile appeared as the two of them had a good laugh.

"I am just fascinated by your eagerness when you eat. You make the food seem so much more than it is."

"Wow, maybe I should do some food commercials. I could

صداقة ידידות صداقة ידידות صداقة ידידות صداقة ידידות

صداقة يديدوت صداقة يديدوت صداقة يديدوت صداقة يديدوت

become really rich, buy a soccer stadium, and we could play forever. How do you like that, Joshua?"

"It's a nice dream …" Joshua's voice trailed off. "Let's not go overboard. I only said I enjoyed watching you eat."

"Are you okay? You suddenly seem sad," Ahmed asked.

"I'm so glad we met, but I'm so sad that this friendship will be short-lived."

"Joshua, don't think of that. Just concentrate on the adventure of finding our wonderful Israeli carpet merchant." Ahmed tried hard to shrug off Joshua's comment, but he knew he was right. *Let's enjoy the moment. This friendship cannot exist until our people live in peace.* Ahmed kept this thought to himself. He genuinely liked Joshua and felt a kindred spirit with him, but he knew the reality of their existence and was resigned to the outcome.

"You boys were certainly hungry. Now you'll get a good start for what you're ready to do. Good luck, Ahmed!" Ima hugged him. "I know you will find your family, but for now, you are part of our family, okay?"

Ahmed looked at Ima, and he could feel the tears forming in the corners of his eyes. He knew she saw them too, but was thoughtful enough not to say anything to him. Mrs. Atai, your kindness has meant so much to me, truly."

"Wait, Ahmed. Ima, did Aba say he had information for us?"

"No not a word. I'm sure he has confidence in both of you to find out what you can. Now go, so you can make the most of this day."

They left the house and walked to their first destination. It was a silent walk as Ahmed thought about his home and everything

صداقة يديدوت صداقة يديدوت صداقة يديدوت صداقة يديدوت

صداقة يدايدوت صداقة يدايدوت صداقة يدايدوت صداقة يدايدوت

he had left behind to search for his family. Oh how he missed his Ommy's home-cooked meals and the smell of his Abi's coffee upon waking and then again after lunch and dinner.

Jiddo's gardens no longer existed, he thought. He wondered if they ever would again. Jiddo was older and didn't have the energy he once had when he and his son began the original plantings. Ahmed missed his conversations with his Abi and his daily words of encouragement. He made Ahmed believe he could conquer anything. *I guess he was right, because I'm on a journey most boys my age wouldn't attempt,* Ahmed said to himself.

Millions of thoughts were racing through his mind when Joshua nudged him along. "Ahmed, are you sleepwalking? We're almost there, so let's be ready when we arrive."

"Oh, sorry. I was just deep in thought. Let's see, you will go in and ask his name and if he knew my Abi. If he recognizes my Abi's name, then signal for me to come in. I'll introduce myself and present my problem to him. If he's not the person, walk out and we will go on to the next merchant."

"Got it!" Joshua announced, holding his hand up to Ahmed for a high five.

As they approached the store, Joshua told Ahmed to wait for the signal. He went inside. Ahmed could see the man approach Joshua from the back, then he saw them talking. The man shook his head and waved his arms in the air. As Joshua walked out, he hung his head down, shaking it back and forth.

"What happened? What's the matter?"

"Old crotchety man, Ahmed. He's definitely not the one. On to the next merchant," Joshua ordered. "This one is a bit further.

صداقة يدايدوت صداقة يدايدوت صداقة يدايدوت صداقة يدايدوت

صداقة يديدوت صداقة يديدوت صداقة يديدوت صداقة يديدوت

We need to turn northwest and walk about six streets over." He sounded like a general giving orders to his troops.

I'm glad he is as persistent as I am, thought Ahmed. "You are a good person, Joshua. I am lucky to have found you."

"And I am lucky to have found you." Joshua chuckled and Ahmed swung his arm around the other's shoulder. After starting out on their walk, a half hour passed, and Joshua began licking his lips.

"Let's stop for a drink. The sun is blazing hot, and we still have a bit to go."

"Okay, Ahmed, good idea. My lips were so dry I wasn't sure how I could even form the words to make conversation."

Thoughts of home and Tulkarm kept racing through Ahmed's mind. The merchants at the market would be busy right now selling their goods, and Abi would normally be on his way back from making his purchases and selling his fruit. Life was good then, but as he looked at Joshua, he just couldn't understand what had happened to his family and their home. He now contrasted that with the kindness of Joshua and his family.

He was confused, but he remembered what his Abi had told him. All Israeli and Palestinian people were not evil. There was a lot of kindness and compassion in these people, and Joshua and his family were proof of this. They opened their home to a complete stranger—and a Palestinian one at that. It was the small factions that created the problems for these communities, impeding any thought of them ever living in harmony.

My friendship with Joshua is an important lesson for me, and I will

صداقة يديدوت صداقة يديدوت صداقة يديدوت صداقة يديدوت

صداقة يدردوت صداقة يدردوت صداقة يدردوت صداقة يدردوت

never forget what I have learned from this experience. It will always be with me, and I will teach it to my children as my Abi had taught it to me.

"Ahmed, here. Grab this bottle and let's go," Joshua yelled to him. "I can see the store from here. We'll do the same thing. You wait out here for the signal."

Ahmed sat down on a bench in front of the furniture store nearby. Joshua went inside but couldn't be seen from the bench.

"Excuse me, sir, is your name Mr. Ben-Horin? You see I have a friend whose father was friends with an Israeli carpet merchant, and he is desperate to find him because he may know how to locate his family." As the gentleman attempted to answer, the two of them heard some shouting outside, and Joshua recognized Ahmed's voice.

He ran to the front of the store and out the door, but he was not fast enough. He saw several police taking off with Ahmed in their car. Joshua called out to him as loudly as he could, and he saw Ahmed turn his head with tears streaming down his face. Joshua continued to scream Ahmed's name until the carpet merchant approached to find out what had happened.

"Young man, calm down," he gently ordered.

"You don't understand. He's my friend, and his parents are missing. Now they've taken him in, for what I don't know, but I'm scared. I have to do something."

"Okay, I understand. Come in and tell me the whole story, and we'll see what we can do."

"No, I have to go to the station where they are taking him and tell them everything. They have to release him. I'll call my Aba. Do you have a phone I can use?"

صداقة يدردوت صداقة يدردوت صداقة يدردوت صداقة يدردوت

صداقة يديدوت صداقة يديدوت صداقة يديدوت صداقة يديدوت

"Yes, yes, of course. Come inside and sit down. You need to settle down so you can be calm when you call him. What did you say your name was?" The gentleman led him into the store and pulled a chair out for him to sit. He left and went to the back of the store.

Upon returning, he brought Joshua a bottle of cold water. "Here, drink this, wipe your brow, and we'll call your Aba."

"Thank you, Mr. … I feel better already."

"My name is Ben-Horin, and you are?"

"Excuse me, my name is Joshua. I must have a clear mind when I call." He took a deep breath and let it out, then said, "Okay, I'm ready."

Joshua and Mr. Ben-Horin walked back into the store. Joshua used the merchant's phone to place his call.

"Speak slowly. You don't want to alarm your Aba."

Just several days ago, life was so simple in Netanya. Well, as simple as it could be without thinking about any attacks as everyone went on with their daily lives. This was a beautiful city with its beaches that attracted so many to it, and its vast skies sheltering the many buildings and homes that had been built there.

Joshua felt fortunate not to wonder where his parents were, but Ahmed was not as blessed as he was. The constant ringing of the phone brought Joshua out of his daydreaming, and then he heard his Aba's message to leave a number.

"Aba, this is Joshua. The police came and took Ahmed, and I don't know why. He's probably at the Ne'urim Police Station. Please meet me there so we can find out what happened. Please, Aba, I beg you. Call me back. I'm afraid for him." He turned to

صداقة يديدوت صداقة يديدوت صداقة يديدوت صداقة يديدوت

صداقة يديدوت صداقة يديدوت صداقة يديدوت صداقة يديدوت

Mr. Ben-Horin and said, "If you don't mind, I will wait here until my Aba calls."

"Sit on the bench and let me know if he calls back and what you are planning to do." Mr. Ben-Horin was a gentle and kind person. Joshua wondered if he would be as gentle and kind knowing where Ahmed came from and why he was in Netanya.

"Sir, I never did explain why I was here with Ahmed, and I want you to know everything."

In his mind, Joshua practiced what he was going to say. *I hope this goes well. People can show you one face until they hear something they don't like, and then they turn on you and treat you like an unwanted stray dog.* He swallowed hard and thought again about being honest with Mr. Ben-Horin.

"So, what is it that you want to tell me, Joshua?" Mr. Ben-Horin asked curiously.

"I just met Ahmed the other day. I was walking in the Gardens, and he was sitting on a bench having a snack when I approached him. After he and I introduced ourselves, he told me why he had come to Netanya from Tulkarm."

"Tulkarm! Then he is not an Israeli. Is he Palestinian? … Of course he's not Israeli—*Ahmed*!"

"Yes, Mr. Ben-Horin, but please listen and don't come to your own conclusions," Joshua pleaded. He proceeded to tell the rest of his story.

"Ahmed's parents had a house that was situated close to where the security wall was being put up. They had been told to vacate before the work was to begin. Several weeks had passed, and the Quessem family continued their daily chores and activities.

صداقة يديدوت صداقة يديدوت صداقة يديدوت صداقة يديدوت

صداقة يديدوت صداقة يديدوت صداقة يديدوت صداقة يديدوت

Ahmed's Abi had no intention of taking his family and leaving their home.

"Ahmed had to deliver a note for his Ommy and when he returned, the house was demolished. There was nothing left, Mr. Ben-Horin, and worse than that, his family was gone. Ahmed knew there was something wrong because his Ommy seemed very anxious about him delivering the note, but he wouldn't question her and show disrespect. He asked everyone in his village where they might be. If they knew, they didn't tell him because of what may have happened to his family.

"After speaking to someone at the marketplace, he believed his Abi may have argued with the soldiers and tried to resist them coming in to demolish the house. He thinks his entire family may have been taken away to prison, but he doesn't know for sure. Ahmed remembered his Abi's good Israeli friend, a carpet merchant in Netanya. Since the local people were of no help to him, he believed with the friend's connections that he could find out what happened to his family and he could help him. But now all that is lost."

"Joshua, this is not a good situation for Ahmed or for you and your family. You know how it is here. You are risking a lot for a boy you have just met. Why are you so passionate about helping him?"

"This is about more than friendship. This is about a person's humanity."

"Well, such a big word for such a young boy." Mr. Ben-Horin seemed impressed by Joshua's compassion. Joshua started to feel he made a mistake by confiding in Mr. Ben-Horin. He didn't want to be placated or made to feel younger than the boy he was.

صداقة يديدوت صداقة يديدوت صداقة يديدوت صداقة يديدوت

صداقة يديدوت صداقة يديدوت صداقة يديدوت صداقة يديدوت

"Never mind. I knew you wouldn't understand. I shouldn't have told you anything. Please forget everything I just said. Somehow I will make this work for Ahmed, even if I have to do it alone. And I'm fifteen, Mr. Ben-Horin. I am not a young boy!" Joshua was insulted but also disappointed at the man's reaction.

"Young sabra, I can see you are strong-willed and determined to help Ahmed, and I believe you will do just that. Wait for your Aba to call, and then you can plan what to do next."

"Thank you for having faith in what I want to do. I am sorry for being disrespectful to you," Joshua said apologetically. The merchant nodded at him and left the room.

Joshua kept checking the clock on the table in the store. He got up and began pacing back and forth, looking at the pictures on the wall that showed previous generations of carpet merchants. Walking around and looking at the beautiful colors and designs on the carpets remaining in the store, Joshua called out to Mr. Ben-Horin.

"What is it Joshua?"

"I was just wondering how long you have been in this business. Are these members of your family?" Joshua asked as he pointed to the pictures on the wall.

"Yes. My family has been in the carpet business for generations. My grandfather came here when Israel was being settled. He and my grandmother escaped from Russia and were excited to be part of the establishment of a homeland for the Jewish people.

"They became members of a kibbutz, but my grandfather always wanted to continue the carpet business that he had established in Russia. When the opportunity came about, he started a small shop

صداقة يديدوت صداقة يديدوت صداقة يديدوت صداقة يديدوت

صداقة يدِيدות صداقة يدِيدות صداقة يدِيدות صداقة يدِيدות

and built a large clientele. Times were good for his business, and it has been true of mine until the department stores took a lot of my business from me.

"Life has changed, Joshua. Since the bombings, it has been difficult for Palestinians to come to Netanya. Some do for work, and there are those who come occasionally to shop. The soldiers can be very troublesome for these people at the checkpoints. Between the wars and the groups of troublemakers who encouraged the hatred and violence that we have seen, the Israeli government had no choice but to intervene. This angered both sides, who now had to be separated like animals from their predators. It is a difficult situation, and without the cooperation of both sides, well, I don't know what will happen."

"Wow, your family was part of such an important history."

At that moment the phone rang, and Mr. Ben-Horin quickly answered it. "Hello. … Yes, he's here. This is Moishe. Dan, how are you? I haven't seen you in a while. How's the carpet business?" Mr. Ben-Horin laughed and continued. "The business has been the same for me. I've gotten rid of most of my inventory, and shortly I'll close the shop. Just a moment; I'll put Joshua on. He's anxious to speak to you. It seems a friend of his is in great trouble with the authorities."

Joshua stood there with his mouth opened, and his eyes as wide as a blue moon. "Mr. Ben-Horin, you know my Aba? Of course, you would. Both of you are in the carpet business. I can't believe all of this." Joshua almost forgot his Aba was waiting to speak to him on the dangling phone that he held. There were just too many

صداقة يدِيدות صداقة يدِيدות صداقة يدِيدות صداقة يدِيدות

coincidences he thought. Too many things happening that seemed as though someone was methodically planning them.

"Hello, Aba. Sorry I messed up. Did you get my message? Ahmed was taken in by the authorities while I was in Mr. Ben-Horin's shop. I don't know what happened. He was waiting for me on a bench outside when I heard yelling. I ran outside only to find Ahmed being put in a vehicle and taken away. I'm so afraid for him. With what happened—"

Mr. Atai stopped Joshua by saying, "Wait, Joshua. Calm down. You don't know what happened. I want you to sit down and think about it. I have to make some phone calls, and I will call you back. Stay with Mr. Ben-Horin. Do not try to do anything by yourself, you understand?"

"Yes, Aba," Joshua promised. He hung up the phone, sat down, and looked like he had lost the most important soccer match of his life.

"Joshua, have faith. Your Aba will help you and your friend. He's a good and honorable man. I have known him for many years, and he will do the right thing for you. He is a peaceful person who doesn't enjoy discord among anyone. Here's some money. Go down to the corner and get some lunch, and while you're at it, bring me back a falafel sandwich. Be sure they don't skip the tahini or the olives. I have some water and juice here. Now go and stay positive. Ahmed is counting on you."

Joshua turned and smiled at Mr. Ben-Horin. He was trying to figure out why he was suddenly so understanding, but he let it go.

As he walked down to the corner, he couldn't stop thinking about Ahmed. *We're wasting too much time. Every minute that goes*

صداقة يديدوت صداقة يديدوت صداقة يديدوت صداقة يديدوت

by could be the end for Ahmed and his family. Who knows what they will do to him. What if they find out about his parents? I should have gone to the authorities myself to explain the situation and not have tried to get Aba involved.

He saw an image of himself in one of the storefront windows and stopped to take a better look. Joshua saw a young man and not the little boy that his Aba thought he was. He began to feel a freedom and confidence that he hadn't known. Joshua started to understand that with the death of his brother, Avram, and as Aba's only remaining son, it was only natural that his Aba wanted to hold him back. By doing so, Aba could hold back the inevitable: joining the Israeli army.

Joshua looked up to see the vendor acknowledging him. "Sorry. Two falafel sandwiches with plenty of tahini and olives, please." The smell of falafel, pita, and spices alerted Joshua to how hungry he really was. He had been so preoccupied with Ahmed that he had forgotten he hadn't eaten since breakfast.

After paying for the lunch, he thanked the vendor and began walking back to Mr. Ben-Horin's shop. He felt like tearing through the wrapping but decided it would be rude to eat without the person who graciously bought his lunch. Joshua had a terrible impatience along with the hunger he felt inside. Mr. Ben-Horin was waiting outside the shop as he approached.

"I'm glad to see you returned. I was getting worried that your young mind might convince you to take this situation on by yourself."

"Mr. Ben-Horin, with all respect to you, you are sounding more

صداقة ידידות صداقة ידידות صداقة ידידות صداقة ידידות

and more like my Aba. Of course, I thought about taking this on, but I realized my Aba could be a great help to me."

"Okay then, let's sit down and eat. Come in the back. I have set everything up for us. I'm sure your Aba will call back as soon as he comes up with a plan."

They walked to the back, and Joshua emptied out the package that contained the falafel. "I made sure you had your tahini and olives." Joshua smiled shyly.

"Thank you, Joshua. This is even better than I usually get." They ate quietly, the hunger taking on more importance than any conversation they could have. As they continued eating, the phone rang.

Joshua sprang up and ran to get the phone call. "Hello, hello. Yes, Mr. Ben-Horin is here. Who is calling, please?" Joshua slowly walked back to the table. "Mrs. Stern is calling about her carpet."

"Thank you. Go ahead, finish your falafel." Joshua could hear the conversation between Mrs. Stern and Mr. Ben-Horin. It sounded like the conversations his Aba had with customers when Joshua would visit the shop to help him out.

The merchant was shaking his head as he made his way to the back of the shop. "Meshugganah, crazy I tell you, Joshua. I just spoke to her yesterday, and she's calling me to ask the same questions I already answered for her. This is a younger woman, but they don't want to hear what I have to say. They only want to hear what they want to hear."

Joshua laughed. He remembered his father having customers like that, and he would come home at the end of the day complaining just like Mr. Ben-Horin.

صداقة ידידות صداقة ידידות صداقة ידידות صداقة ידידות

صداقة يديدوت صداقة يديدوت صداقة يديدوت صداقة يديدوت

"Enough of that. Let's finish this delicious lunch, okay, sabra?"

"You bet." Just then Joshua looked down at the empty wrapper, realizing his lunch was finished."

"Hungry boy, weren't you?" Mr. Ben-Horin chuckled. Again, the phone rang, and Mr. Ben-Horin held his arm out with the palm of his hand down to keep Joshua in his chair. He walked to where the phone was and picked it up.

"Hello, Dan. Yes, he's here. We were just finishing lunch." He called to Joshua, "Your Aba is on the phone."

Joshua ran toward the phone and grabbed it from Mr. Ben-Horin's hand. "Hello, Aba, did you find out anything? Do you have a plan?"

"Joshua, listen to me. Think clearly and without anxiety." Dan tried to calm his son down before he gave him his decision. "I have thought this over very carefully, and I have decided we should not get involved in this situation. The authorities will hear what Ahmed has to say, question him, check out his identification, and send him back to Tulkarm. I know how these things go."

"No, Aba, that's not how these things go. His family has been taken away, and once they find that out and the reason why, they will do the same to him. I knew I should have done this on my own." Joshua frantically raised his voice to his father.

"Joshua, I'm coming to get you. Stay there with Mr. Ben-Horin and don't do anything foolish. I'll be there as soon as I can." And with that, Mr. Atai hung up the phone.

Joshua slammed down the phone and called out to Mr. Ben-Horin, thanking him for the lunch and his company, then ran out of the shop. After hearing the conversation between Joshua and his

صداقة يديدوت صداقة يديدوت صداقة يديدوت صداقة يديدوت

صداقة يديدوت صداقة يديدوت صداقة يديدوت صداقة يديدوت

Aba, Mr. Ben-Horin was alerted to his anger and frustration. He walked as fast as he could to catch up with him, but Joshua's youth was no match for the older man.

When he got to the door, he yelled out for Joshua to come back. His cries were ignored as Joshua disappeared down the street. Mr. Ben-Horin shook his head and turned to go back into the store. *These young people—so foolish thinking they can change thousands of years of hatred and discontent.*

"Hello, Dan, it's Moishe. Your son has taken off, and I'm afraid he's going to get involved in something that will spiral out of control. I tried to stop him, but he was too fast for me and ran down the street, ignoring my pleas. I feel so bad that we have to communicate under these circumstances. Why don't you come down to the shop, and we'll figure out what to do?"

"Thanks, Moishe. You are a good friend. I'm on my way."

صداقة يديدوت صداقة يديدوت صداقة يديدوت صداقة يديدوت

Chapter 7

Joshua stopped for a moment to catch his breath after running for what seemed like miles. He wasn't sure which station Ahmed was taken to, but he had to think about which one would make the most sense. After stopping at the vendor across the street to get a drink, he sat down on a nearby bench. He was close enough to continue his walk near the beach where he knew one of the stations was located.

Joshua began to feel relaxed as he looked at the sky that radiated a blue so intense his eyes couldn't move away from its gaze. It had a calming effect on him. He finished his drink and began to get up, but hesitated. *Maybe this is the way it has to be; maybe Aba is right. Ahmed will be sent back to Tulkarm and that will be the end of it.*

His thought was replaced with knowing that if he did nothing, he was as guilty as anyone else who has shown hatred and a lack of compassion to the Palestinians. Again, he was swayed to believe that he had already shown kindness and compassion; however, a gnawing anxiety in the bottom of his stomach propelled him out of the bench, and he began his walk to the station near the beach.

"I've come this far; I can't let Ahmed down. He's counting on me." Joshua's determination hurried his steps toward his destination.

Back at the shop of Mr. Ben-Horin, Dan Atai arrived and turned the handle on the door only to find it locked. He went to ring the bell, but stopped when he saw Moishe Ben-Horin walking toward the door smiling. Moishe unlocked the door and both wrapped their arms around one another.

"Shalom, my dear friend. It's so good to see you, even with what we have to deal with today."

"Shalom to you," Dan returned the greeting. "It's been too long. I guess we've both been busy making a living." Dan gave out a barely audible and uncomfortable laugh.

"How about a cup of coffee? Let's go to the back and sit down," Moishe offered.

"Sounds good. I need to sit down." Dan Atai seemed tired and defeated. He was an unusually patient and forgiving man, but this afternoon, his age got the better of him. They walked to the back of the shop without words spoken. Moishe pulled out a chair for him.

"How do you like your coffee, Dan?"

"Just some sugar, please. I don't want to appear rude, Moishe, but I need to find Joshua before I have my hands full with the authorities. I hope you will forgive me."

"My goodness," Moishe replied, "an apology is not necessary. With what is going on, I should not have wasted your time with a cup of coffee."

"Thank you."

"Without spending another minute here, why don't we drive to the station to locate your son. We'll start with the closest one to my shop and work our way to the others."

"Moishe, I appreciate your willingness to help, but you don't need to get involved in this. Joshua started it, and now I will finish it for him. He's too young to understand that this can get

صداقة ידידות صداقة ידידות صداقة ידידות صداقة ידידות

very complicated for Ahmed and his family and all of us. He's emotional, hardheaded, and impulsive—a bad combination for a teenager. The authorities will not appreciate what he is trying to do, nor will they sympathize with his willingness to help a stranger, especially a Palestinian who should not be in Netanya.

"I know Joshua feels a friendship with this boy, but it's only been two days. He's strong-willed—a lot like me, but not as easygoing." Dan let out a laugh and patted Moishe on his back. At that moment, they embraced one another.

"Well, strong-willed or not, I'm going with you and that's that. No more talk. Let's go and confront this situation. The authorities don't know who they're dealing with. They'll get twice as much trouble for their time, ha!" Dan knew Moishe very well and realized he wouldn't be able to talk him out of helping.

"Okay, my friend, let's go," Dan ordered, and Moishe's grin grew wide. He knew he won this battle and didn't know if he would be as successful helping Dan and Joshua.

Moishe locked the front door, and they walked to the back door to get to his car. He put his hand on Dan's shoulder. "We've seen a lot in our lifetime, haven't we? This country was young when our grandparents arrived. It was an exciting time, and there was so much to be accomplished, but they never gave up. So why should we feel defeated now? There's been turmoil and violence in our lives, and you have known the worst of it. You've survived because you are a strong sabra. Whatever we have to do, we will get it done."

Moishe was trying to remain positive in a situation that could turn very ugly. Dan listened patiently and quietly got in the car. The ride to the station was uncomfortably silent. Moishe didn't want to

صداقة ידידות صداقة ידידות صداقة ידידות صداقة ידידות

overstep the boundary of his friendship with Dan, and he tried to make some light conversation. "How is the wife, Dan? Still busy with the gallery?"

"She has been working very hard with the current exhibition of American artists. She's been obsessive about her work ever since Avram—"

"Dan, you don't have to," Moishe interrupted.

"It's all right, Moishe. This is her reaction in dealing with her pain. Mine has been more introspective and quiet. Believe it or not, I feel peaceful and calm now. I have a new appreciation for all people. Does that make sense to you? Adiva makes me think I have lost my mind. She doesn't think I should feel the way I do. We have reacted to Avram's death in very different ways, but it doesn't mean one of us is wrong in how we're feeling. We are each reacting in a way that makes sense to us."

"Dan, please don't revisit this. You're not crazy, and you have to do whatever it is that gives you peace and a way to move on and live your life. Adiva must do the same. Even if you both react differently, it shouldn't pull you apart. There's so much we can't change, but there are things we can do to allow ourselves to cope. You and Adiva are remarkable people, remember that."

"Your words of support mean so much. Thank you."

The trip to the station continued in a silence that acknowledged the need for both Moishe and Dan to sit and reflect about the events that had unfolded. Moishe began looking for parking at the station and pulled into a parking space a short distance from the front door. Dan opened his door and waited for his friend. They

صداقة يديدوت صداقة يديدوت صداقة يديدوت صداقة يديدوت

walked to the front of the station, where they were greeted by a magistrate.

"Shalom, gentlemen. How can I help you today?"

"This is Dan Atai and I am Moishe Ben-Horin." Moishe took the liberty of introducing both of them. At that moment, Moishe heard his name called in the distance. He turned and saw BenjaminYehuda walking toward him.

"What are you doing here? In trouble with the authorities?" Ben joked. He wrapped his arms around his friend. "It is so good to see you. Can I help with anything?"

"Perhaps, but let me introduce you to a friend of mine, Dan Atai. He owns the carpet shop on Gad Machnes Street."

"Shalom, Dan. Good to meet you."

"Benjamin is one of the community volunteers, Dan. He's been doing this for many years."

"Shalom to you," Dan responded.

"Listen, Ben, it's a long story, but I think you may be able to help."

Ben held out his arm to direct them to his office. "Come and let's talk in private." They followed Ben into his office and sat down across from the desk. It was a small, cramped office—one of several reserved for the volunteers like Ben. There were many family pictures on the desk and volunteer awards lined the wall behind the desk.

"A nice domain you have here, Ben," Moishe teased. "Not bad for over twenty years of service, right?"

"This office shows you how valued we are," Ben replied sarcastically. "Enough of that, how can I help you, Dan?"

صداقة يديدوت صداقة يديدوت صداقة يديدوت صداقة يديدوت

صداقة ‬ידידות صداقة ‬ידידות صداقة ‬ידידות صداقة ‬ידידות

Dan looked at Moishe. His eyes communicated to him to please begin the explanation. Dan's facial lines appeared deeper than they had earlier, and it was clear that Joshua had added a few years to his life in the last few hours.

Moishe placed his hand on Dan's arm and began to tell Ben what had brought them to the station. "Dan's son, Joshua, who is fifteen years old, was walking in the Gardens several days ago and met a young man whom he befriended. That may seem simple enough, but the boy is a Palestinian from Tulkarm. He came to Netanya in the hope of finding an Israeli friend of his father who could help him.

"The family's home was demolished because of its proximity to the wall being erected. When the boy came home from an errand, everything had been torn down and the people in his community that he asked gave out little if no information to him. Whether they were frightened for their own security, no one knows. The boy was desperate and didn't know what to do. He panicked and managed to get past the checkpoint safely and without suspicion because of two gentlemen who pretended to be his relatives. He and Joshua decided they would check the police stations to find out if his family was arrested and brought to Netanya.

"That is where I come in. They stopped in to my shop to see if I was the merchant the boy was trying to locate. While Joshua was talking to me, there was a ruckus outside, and when he ran out to see what was going on, the police had the boy in the car and sped away. Joshua was afraid for his friend, and when Dan called and told him that the boy would be sent back to Tulkarm and he should let it go, Joshua took off to find the police station where his friend

صداقة ‬ידידות صداقة ‬ידידות صداقة ‬ידידות صداقة ‬ידידות

صداقة يدىدوت صداقة يدىدوت صداقة يدىدوت صداقة يدىدوت

was taken. This was our first stop because we don't know which station he is in." Moishe sat back and waited for a response.

"That's quite a story, my friend. You both know the authorities do not take it lightly when a Palestinian is found without a legitimate purpose in Netanya. A young boy alone raises even more suspicion."

"Yes we do, Ben, that's why Dan looks so troubled. We need to find Joshua before more trouble develops." There was quiet, and Moishe and Dan took the opportunity to look over the pictures on the desk.

"What would you do, Mr. Yehuda, if it was your child?" Dan said as he looked at the happy faces of children in the pictures.

"This is what we will do!" Ben commanded, breaking the quiet that took over the office. "First, I will find out who they are holding here, or maybe they can tell me what they know about anything going on at the other stations. If he's not here and I can't find out any information, then I will call each station to try and locate him. I will then ask about the boy and his family. What are their names, please?" Moishe and Dan felt reassured and thanked Ben for whatever help he could give.

"The boy is Ahmed Quessem. I don't know the parents' names. Thank you, Ben. Let's pray for the best," Dan said and seemed more alert now.

"Both of you wait here, and I will see what I can find out. I'll come back as quickly as possible."

A young woman came in and asked if they would like something to drink. Water seemed like the only reasonable beverage for nervous stomachs. "Some water, please," Moishe answered for himself and Dan. A few minutes later, the bottled water was brought in.

صداقة يدىدوت صداقة يدىدوت صداقة يدىدوت صداقة يدىدوت

صداقة يديدות صداقة يديدوت صداقة يديدوت صداقة يديدوت

Dan got up and began walking around the small space that was available. He went over to the window and looked out at the street behind Ben's office.

"Simple is good," he said under his breath.

"What, Dan?"

"A childish thought, nothing."

"You can tell me, childish or not."

"It's just that having a simple life is really a good thing."

"And you think your life is complicated right now, yes?" He wanted to lend support, but didn't want Dan to think he was merely being polite. "Dan, this is a temporary situation. It is only a complication, and we will resolve it. Then your life will go back to simple. By the way, what is your secret for a simple life, because mine isn't anywhere close to being simple? So tell me your secret."

"I thought you were taking me seriously, but now I see you think this is funny, eh? I know I'm being unrealistic, but I was comparing simple to what is going on now."

Ben walked in smiling. "The good news is that I have found him—that is, I found your son. He's at the community center station near Ovadya Gardens. He created quite a scene, but they calmed him down. I asked them to please keep him until we get there."

"Mr. Yehuda, I am grateful."

"Please call me Ben. Let's see what we can find out and if we can help Joshua's friend. What's his name again, Ahmed?"

"It's Ahmed Quessem. That's all I know. He's a lovely boy. We opened our home to him. His friendship with Joshua seems genuine and sincere, but you never can be sure, can you?"

صداقة يديدوت صداقة يديدوت صداقة يديدوت صداقة يديدوت

صداقة يديدوت صداقة يديدوت صداقة يديدوت صداقة يديدوت

"Genuine or not, the authorities will not be impressed. We'll try and appeal to their sense of humanity. That is, if they have any left after some of the things they have witnessed."

Dan responded by saying, "Ben, we cannot keep indicting everyone like that. Ahmed is a good person. He seems to have enough idealism in him to even like Joshua and me." Dan wanted to be positive about the outcome for both Joshua and Ahmed.

Ben stared at him, seeming to be in deep thought. "Don't make light of this, Dan. While the way we feel may be admirable, you know as well as I do that many do not feel the same way, especially when it comes to the authorities and civil guard volunteers such as myself. Some of them have lost family members, but they are not as forgiving as you."

Dan took Ben's message as a truth that was too evident in the community. Why did he continue to believe in the fairness that he felt human beings still held on to?

Ben led them out of the building, waving over to where his car was parked. "It's a short ride to the center. In the meantime, let's discuss our strategy for presenting the situation." Ben seemed to have a greater interest in this than Dan and Moishe.

On the way to the center, Dan and Moishe looked at the many places they hadn't seen in a while. "I haven't been to Ovadya Gardens in many months. I remember spending a lot of time there when I was a boy." Dan looked at Moishe for a response, but Moishe sat quietly as he had at the end of their visit to Ben's office.

"Netanya is a beautiful city. I should take more time to study the many sights and architecture and visit the beach. The beach was always a great place to think about my life and the goals I had set

صداقة يديدوت صداقة يديدوت صداقة يديدوت صداقة يديدوت

صداقة يديدوت صداقة يديدوت صداقة يديدوت صداقة يديدوت

for myself. Such innocence is good. Age can hold you back because you become aware of the pitfalls in everything. A young boy feels he can conquer anything. I guess that's how Joshua feels now." With that thought, Ben asked if they had thought about their approach with the authorities.

"Ben, with your experience, you may be the best person to advise us about how to begin."

"First I would deal with Joshua and his situation with them. Then I would state the absolute facts of what happened with Ahmed's family and how your son met Ahmed. Leave it up to them to decide the next step. If I have to, I will step in. Does that make sense to you? Are we in agreement?"

"Absolutely. It makes sense and I will follow your advice, but feel free to interrupt whenever you think it's necessary," Dan said. Moishe nodded his head in agreement.

Ben then announced that they had arrived. He drove into the officials' parking area and placed his identification on the windshield. "Okay everyone, let's go." Dan got out of the car and asked them to wait a few minutes; he had to take a short walk just to glimpse the gardens he hadn't seen in a while.

"Two minutes, Dan, that's all. I have to get back to my office sometime today."

He walked up the street to Ovadya Gardens. They were even more beautiful than he remembered and busy with old men playing chess and loudly discussing political issues. Children and parents were buying snacks at the falafel vendors, and young mothers with their strollers were taking their babies for a much needed daily walk. Whatever happened in Netanya, life went on just as he

صداقة يديدوت صداقة يديدوت صداقة يديدوت صداقة يديدوت

صداقة ידידות صداقة ידידות صداقة ידידות صداقة ידידות

remembered it as a young boy. He turned to head back to Ben and Moishe and saw them waiting in the distance.

"Did you find what you were looking for?" Moishe asked.

"I wasn't looking for something. I just wanted to revisit some memories."

"Capturing your youth? If we could only do that!" Ben acknowledged.

"Make fun all you want. There's nothing wrong with going back in time and revisiting happy memories, now is there, gentlemen?" Dan couldn't help but be defensive, and he felt nervous about seeing Joshua after telling him to forget about his friend. "Let's go in and get this done."

Ben seemed confident about a good outcome for everyone. Dan and Moishe did not feel the same way. Moishe had a good relationship with the community police and knew some of the civilian volunteers, but he had a nagging feeling that he and Dan might not get to enjoy the sunshine for a while. Once the authorities became suspicious, they could keep Dan and Moishe as long as they needed to.

As Ben walked in, he greeted several gentlemen who were standing and having an intense conversation. The others in the room looked at Dan and Moishe as strangers who were intruders in their building. Dan leaned against Moishe and gave him a gentle shove, looking at him with uncertainty. Moishe shook his head and rolled his eyes toward Dan and walked closer to Ben.

"Gentlemen, this is Dan Atai and Moishe Ben-Horin, good friends of mine. ... Dan, Moishe, this is Abe Bronfman and Meshek Geller, constables at the community center."

صداقة ידידות صداقة ידידות صداقة ידידות صداقة ידידות

صداقة يديدوت صداقة يديدوت صداقة يديدوت صداقة يديدوت

As the men shook hands, Meshek asked what brought them to the center. "I hope it's nothing serious," Meshek offered.

Ben interrupted, "Nothing serious, but I think it's a good idea if we could sit down and discuss this."

"Very well, come this way. Mind you, from the look on all your faces, I'm not convinced that this is nothing serious." Meshek looked at Ben and the others with his eyebrows tightly creased and the pupils of his eyes barely visible. They walked down a long hall that was lined with pictures of past constables, sergeants, and other notables.

"This way." Abe opened the door and allowed his guests to enter first. "Please, have a seat. Can I get anyone a bottle of water?" Without waiting for an answer, he went to the small refrigerator behind his desk and brought out three bottles of water and placed them on his desk.

"Now, what is the problem, gentlemen—and I assume there is a problem, yes?" Meshek asked. No one took the initiative to begin, and Dan and Moishe didn't understand why Ben wasn't stepping up as he said he would.

"Listen, I would like to help if I can, but let's cut to the chase. Would someone please tell me what it is I am supposed to do to help you? Don't waste my time!" The gracious host became the hardened constable who had witnessed and been involved in much greater situations and conflicts than he was about to get involved in today. Dan felt Meshek's patience had been tested and worn out over time in dealing with Palestinian conflicts.

Ben took the lead. "Meshek, Abe, we are sorry and don't mean to waste your time. I wasn't sure where to begin, so I'll just tell

صداقة يديدوت صداقة يديدوت صداقة يديدوت صداقة يديدوت

صداقة يديدوت صداقة يديدوت صداقة يديدوت صداقة يديدوت

you the story as it unfolded. Dan's son Joshua was walking in the Gardens when he saw a boy about his age eating some lunch. He walked over to him, introduced himself, and they started talking about themselves. They found they had a lot in common, and Joshua called his Ima to ask if the boy could come for dinner. Dan and his wife were gracious enough to open their home to this boy whom Joshua had just met.

"It turned out the boy, Ahmed, was from Tulkarm. He had traveled by bus with two gentlemen who had permission to do business in Netanya. When they arrived, he decided to go off on his own."

"Okay, but there must be more than this or you wouldn't be here, right, Ben?" Abe asked.

"Yes, yes, of course there's more. Let me go on."

"Sorry for the interruption. Please, continue," Meshek added as an apology for Abe.

"Ahmed didn't just want to take a ride to Netanya—wait. Let me go back a bit. Perhaps I should have started earlier in the story. Anyway, Ahmed's family home had the unfortunate fate to be built near the wall that is now being erected. His father and grandfather had built the home, so it held an especially sacred place in their hearts and family history. After several weeks, Ahmed's mother and father had said nothing to him about the situation and sent him on a long errand, knowing that when he got back, the home may or may not have been standing.

"I'm sure they felt it would still be there when he returned. However, he came back to a pile of rubble with security soldiers watching as the debris was taken away. Ahmed panicked and ran

صداقة يديدوت صداقة يديدوت صداقة يديدوت صداقة يديدوت

صداقة يديدوت صداقة يديدوت صداقة يديدوت صداقة يديدوت

to every merchant he knew in the marketplace to find out where his parents were. If they knew, they were not talking and told him not to worry. His parents would be back for him."

Ben turned to Dan. "How am I doing so far with the story; is it accurate?"

"You're doing a splendid job describing the situation," Dan said.

"You know how impatient and impulsive young boys can be. He wasn't willing to wait around, and he came up with a plan to travel to Netanya to find an Israeli friend of his father's. He thought this man could help in locating his family, whom he believed had been taken to a local police station in Netanya. He was smart enough to befriend two older men who were traveling to Netanya and went with them to the checkpoint to get on the bus. When he arrived, he walked to the Gardens, got some lunch, and met Joshua. Excuse me." Ben opened the bottle of water and embraced it for the much-needed fluid. He quickly drank most of it and set the bottle down on the desk.

"Ahmed had dinner with the Atai family and spent the night. He and Joshua hatched a plan to find this Israeli carpet merchant. Mr. Atai gave them the names of the various shopkeepers, and they began their search this morning. Everything was going smoothly until Joshua went to Mr. Ben-Horin's shop to ask him if he knew Ahmed's father. Outside they heard arguing and shouting, and by the time Joshua ran out to see what was going on, Ahmed had been taken away in a police car."

"So that is it?" Abe asked. "You want me to check on this boy Ahmed to see if he has been brought in?"

"Yes … no, that is not the whole story." Ben wasn't sure where

صداقة يديدوت صداقة يديدوت صداقة يديدوت صداقة يديدوت

صداقة ידידות صداقة ידידות صداقة ידידות صداقة ידידות

he wanted to continue, but he knew the urgency in finding both Joshua and Ahmed. "Joshua was frantic and called Dan. Dan asked Joshua to stay calm until he thought it over to come up with a plan. When Dan called back, he told Joshua to forget about finding Ahmed. The authorities would hear his story, find out he is a citizen in Tulkarm, and send him back.

"Joshua wanted nothing to do with that plan, so he took off for all the police stations to find his friend. I called some people I know, and they told me he was here, so here we are. That's the story, all of it. Now can you help us?"

Meshek turned to Dan. "You know, Mr. Atai, working at the station and trying to keep our citizens secure, I can't help wondering what the real reason is for all this concern about a Palestinian boy who is, shall I say, rightfully a stranger to all of you. What is the fascination with this boy? After all, you are asking for my help, and I believe I have a right to ask you this question. So, can you tell me, please?"

There was a moment of uncomfortable silence. Dan held his head down as though trying to figure out how to respond correctly to Meshek's inquiry.

"Well, Mr. Atai, do you have a reason or has this interest been created by your son?"

"No … of course not. I wanted to do the right thing for this boy. He has done nothing."

"Nothing, really? May I remind you how many times young Palestinian boys have thrown rocks at our soldiers and have been found to carry weapons? You do remember those times don't you,

صداقة يديدوت صداقة يديدوت صداقة يديدوت صداقة يديدوت

Mr. Atai?" Meshek almost seemed to take delight in reminding Dan of these facts.

As he said those words, the smirk across Meshek's face swelled up condescendingly. Ben-Horin and Bronfman said nothing during the exchange and allowed these two to continue with what was beginning to become a war of words.

"With all due respect, Mr. Geller, I know perfectly well what you are talking about. I lost a son in the Israeli army because of a few who hate …" Dan's voice trailed off, but he found the strength to continue. "I don't want to have a debate about this. The boy did nothing. My son befriended him; he slept and ate in my home; we said our prayers together. He has been frantic about his parents as you or I would be. He is not a terrorist but a boy searching for the family he had. That is his only crime, if you want to call him a criminal. Is that enough to arrest him and keep him from being released? Well, is it?"

"Look, Mr. Atai, I have to do my job. If I make a mistake, it could cost our people their lives. Give me a moment, please." As Meshek walked out the door, he turned, hesitating for a moment. He looked closely at Dan Atai and said, "I also offer my condolences to you and your family. I didn't know about your son. We thank him for his service to Israel." Dan looked up but said nothing. Meshek continued to walk down the hall.

"Well that was a pleasant exchange, wasn't it?" Ben-Horin tried to make light of the situation, but Dan wasn't responding.

Abe added, "Mr. Atai, please understand that what Meshek said to you wasn't personal. It's part of our job to be sure that we don't put our citizens in jeopardy. You know how easy it is to have

صداقة يديدوت صداقة يديدوت صداقة يديدوت صداقة يديدوت

صداقة يديدوت صداقة يديدوت صداقة يديدوت صداقة يديدوت

one slipup; it can take the lives of innocent people." That was the first time Abe Bronfman initiated any real conversation.

"I just want to say one thing and that's all. When are we going to stop indicting a whole population of people? You and I both know it is a group of troublemakers who continue to perpetuate this hatred and these horrific incidents. It's not children like Ahmed, I can tell you that." Dan felt the anger of thirty years in the making building up in him.

Footsteps coming closer alerted them to Meshek's return. The only thing missing was another set or two of footsteps.

"Good news, gentlemen. Dan, Joshua is here, and Ahmed is being held in another detention room as are his parents. I'm having Joshua brought in shortly. We can discuss Ahmed when your son arrives."

"Thank you, Mr. Geller."

"Have a seat while we wait for him. Can I get you anything—coffee, tea, water?" Dan did not respond.

"We're fine, thanks," Ben-Horin said.

"Excuse us for a moment, gentlemen," Meshek called out as he and Abe walked out of the office.

Ben-Horin turned to address Dan. "You are a great Aba, and you are doing the right thing for your son. I would do exactly what you are doing. You are a decent human being who always sees the good in people. Meshek and Bronfman have been hardened by what they have seen and the people they have interrogated. It's difficult for them to look beyond the evil they have known. You do understand, don't you?" Moishe tried to offer some clarity to the

صداقة يديدות صداقة يديدות صداقة يديدות صداقة يديدות

situation they were facing, but Dan continued to sit quietly, staring vacantly at the door as he waited for Joshua to walk through it.

Coming out of a self-imposed trance, Dan looked at Moishe and put his arm around him. "You are a true friend and a decent human being too. For you to spend your day with me and give up your time in your business speaks very highly of you. You are a true mensch." Dan stared at Moishe and gave him a hug and smile that showed he meant every word he said.

Moishe smiled back and squeezed Dan's hand. "Everything will be all right." Dan believed it would be.

Just then the door opened, and Joshua came running when he saw his Aba. Dan stood up and embraced his son. They hugged and kissed one another. In the background, Meshek and Abe smiled approvingly. Dan let go of Joshua and walked over to Abe and Meshek and extended his hand. Abe extended his first and then Meshek. "Thank you both for your time and for keeping my son safe."

Meshek said, "Joshua, please sit down. I want you to tell us what you know about this new friend of yours, Ahmed. We need to know as much as we can before we bring him and his family out. Do you think you can do that for us?"

"Yes sir. I'll try my best to tell you what I know." Joshua was given a bottle of juice, and he began to tell the story of how he first met Ahmed. In between questions from both Abe and Meshek, his Aba also had many questions to ask. By the end of the conversation, Bronfman and Geller seemed satisfied.

The two men pulled Dan away from Joshua. "Everything he has told us parallels most of what you said, and it seems legitimate.

صداقة يديدות صداقة يديدوت صداقة يديدوت صداقة يديدوت

صداقة ידידות صداقة ידידות صداقة ידידות صداقة ידידות

Dan, come in this office next door with me. I'd like to speak to you in private."

Meshek and Dan entered the office, and Meshek said, "Security is still checking Ahmed's parents. I can't promise you I will release the parents, but I can bring them out so Ahmed can see that they're okay. Should the parents be cleared, we would take them back to Tulkarm to their apartment. If you are willing, I can turn Ahmed over to you for the time being until we find out more about the parents' background and intentions. I'll explain later. Are you willing to assume responsibility for this boy? I would be very surprised if you said no, based on what you told me earlier. Yes?"

"Of course I'll assume responsibility. Where would he go, spend the night here like a prisoner? I'll sign whatever papers I need to. Please bring him out."

"Good. I'll get the necessary papers ready, give him his identification papers, and Abe will go and get him. Then we'll bring his parents in after you have had an opportunity to tell him where he will be going." Dan didn't know why but Meshek seemed to show a bit more humanity than he first thought. At least it was more visible now.

The two returned to office where the others still sat. "Abe, go get the boy and bring him here."

"Aba, they're getting Ahmed? Will he have to stay here? What's going to happen to him?" Joshua frantically pulled on his Aba's arm.

"Joshua, sit down and stay calm, please." Joshua obeyed his Aba by sitting down and pushing down on the seat with his hands to get the energy out of his body.

"Listen carefully. Ahmed will be coming home with us until

صداقة ידידות صداقة ידידות صداقة ידידות صداقة ידידות

صداقة يديدوت صداقة يديدوت صداقة يديدوت صداقة يديدوت

his parents are released. You will be the brother to him like yours was to you. Take care of him and don't let him get into any trouble. Both of you are to stay at the house. You can go out to the courtyard to play soccer, but that's all, understand? This is serious business, and not a game that we're playing. I *can't* and *will not* go through this again. Do you hear me?"

"Yes Aba. I will take very good care of him. Don't worry. I want him to be with his family and go back to Tulkarm to the life he once knew. He does not belong in a detention center, and I don't ever want him to go back to one again."

"Thank you. I know you are an intelligent boy and understand the seriousness of what has happened." Dan felt relieved that his son had learned a valuable lesson about his country and his people, but even more so, Joshua had learned the lessons his father had taught him about compassion for people. For that, he was most proud of Joshua.

Meshek turned to see Ahmed standing in the doorway, saying nothing. Joshua restrained himself from being boisterous. "Come in, son," Meshek ordered without the gruffness he usually had in his voice. Ahmed slowly stepped into the office, and Joshua stood up and smiled. Ahmed's mouth turned upward, and his steps grew faster and steadier. He and Joshua were face-to-face and hugged one another.

In a faint voice, Ahmed called to Mr. Atai. Dan walked over to Ahmed to shake his hand. "Shalom, assalamalakim, Ahmed." Ahmed's eyes widened and brightened at the sound of Mr. Atai's greeting.

"Mr. Bronfman and I will leave all of you for a short time so

صداقة يديدوت صداقة يديدوت صداقة يديدوت صداقة يديدوت

صداقة يددوت صداقة يديدوت صداقة يديدوت صداقة يديدوت

that you can get reacquainted and speak to Ahmed about your plans," Meshek offered.

Dan's attention turned to Meshek. "Thank you."

"Ahmed, Joshua, sit down please. I was telling Joshua that you will be coming home with us until your parents are released. There is some minor problem that needs to be resolved before they release them," Dan lied. "So until then, you and Joshua will be brothers. You may have to accompany Joshua to soccer camp if you are still with us when it begins. Is that okay with you, Ahmed?" He had a big grin on his face, knowing how much Joshua and Ahmed loved soccer.

"Mr. Atai, I think you are telling a joke now? Of course, I would love to go to camp with Joshua so I can score more points than him in every game!"

"Ha, don't be so sure of yourself, my little brother." Joshua shot back.

"After I sign some papers and we leave, I will take you boys to dinner. Maybe we can meet Ima at the restaurant. We'll try to go to one near the gallery. How does that sound?" Joshua and Ahmed gave a high five to show their excitement.

"Mr. Atai, if I could have another set of parents, I would choose you and Mrs. Atai. You have been so kind and generous. It was a lucky day for me when I met Joshua on the bench." Ahmed held his arm out to shake Mr. Atai's hand. "Thank you for everything."

Ben-Horin nudged at Dan and whispered, "I told you, you did the right thing."

"Ben-Horin, I don't believe you met our new friend, Ahmed

صداقة يديدوت صداقة يديدوت صداقة يديدوت صداقة يديدوت

صداقة يديدوت صداقة يديدوت صداقة يديدوت صداقة يديدوت

Quessem. Ahmed, this is Mr. Ben-Horin, the carpet merchant whose store you never got to see."

"Sir, it is an honor to meet you, and I apologize for this incident that caused so much disruption in your day."

"Nonsense, it is a pleasure to meet you. You gave me some much needed excitement in my day. Besides, I haven't seen Dan Atai in a while, and we have been able to spend such quality time together, right Dan?"

"Uh, yes, that is true. We have had some meaningful conversations today. So thank you, Ahmed. Such a polite young man, not like the young ones I see in the streets shown on television."

Ahmed didn't totally understand what Mr. Ben-Horin had said, but he knew it was an insult against people like him. He was about to say something, when Bronfman abruptly opened the door announcing, "We're bringing the parents now." Ahmed gave Dan a puzzled look.

"What's the matter, Ahmed?"

"Where's my jiddo? Why isn't he with them? What happened to him? And my sister?"

"Ahmed, when your parents get here, you can ask them. I'm sure they'll be able to tell you."

Ahmed's eyebrows quivered in a nervous twitch, and he couldn't keep his lips from shaking. He sat there patiently waiting for his parents. He heard footsteps coming and attempted to jump up. Dan put his hand on Ahmed's shoulder indicating that he should stay seated.

Then the door opened, and there stood Ahmed's parents. They ran to him and held him as tightly as they both could. They were

صداقة يديدوت صداقة يديدوت صداقة يديدوت صداقة يديدوت

صداقة ידידות صداقة ידידות صداقة ידידות صداقة ידידות

all crying and hugging when Meshek walked over and asked them to sit down. As Ahmed's father pulled a chair over closer to the group, he and Dan Atai's eyes met.

Dan froze and he shook his head, almost trying to shake away the vision of who was standing before him. A look of horror came upon both their faces, but neither said anything. Ahmed and Joshua both noticed the look that passed between their fathers but didn't say anything. They stayed transfixed on them to see what would happen next.

Ahmed was the first to speak. "Abi, I would like you to meet the wonderful family who has taken care of me, Mr. Atai and his son, Joshua."

Mr. Quessem stood up and walked to where Dan Atai was sitting. As he put his hand out to shake Dan's, he looked at Dan with a seriousness that frightened both Ahmed and Joshua. "You will be blessed, Mr. Dan Atai, for taking such good care of my son, Ahmed. I am so very pleased to meet you. It is a genuine honor."

As he said those last words, Mr. Quessem's face held a huge smile, and Dan returned the smile. After a few uncomfortable moments, Mr. Quessem released his hand from Dan's. *What a strange exchange*, Joshua thought, but he quickly let the thought go.

Mrs. Quessem stayed seated, and her husband introduced his wife to everyone. Then he looked at Ahmed and said, "I know what you're thinking, my son. Where is your jiddo and Ayat? He and Ayat are fine and in Tulkarm staying with family—which is where you should have gone. You are an adventurer whose curiosity and temper could have gotten you in trouble. You were fortunate this

صداقة ידידות صداقة ידידות صداقة ידידות صداقة ידידות

صداقة يديدوت صداقة يديدوت صداقة يديدوت صداقة يديدوت

time for meeting the Atai family, but don't let your luck run out or there could be very serious consequences."

"Yes, Abi, I promise, but I was so worried about you and Ommy, and I couldn't possibly think about anything but both of you. When will you and Ommy be released so we can go home?" The thought of living at Joshua's house was a pleasant one, but Ahmed's heart was to be where his parents were.

"I can't answer that question, but know this. As soon as we are released, we will contact the Atais and take you home. Be patient. We will be together again. Praise Allah."

"Yes, Abi. I will be patient."

Meshak spoke up. "Dan, I'd like to speak to you in the other room, please. First, you need to sign some papers, and then we can talk." Dan proceeded to follow Meshek into the other office. "Please close the door. This is only for your ears and mine. There was a problem with the Quessem family, which is why they were brought here in the first place. One of the soldiers allegedly heard Mr. Quessem threaten to blow them up. He was heard saying that he had some friends who were bringing explosives to the site where the demolition was going on.

"We're still investigating since this was the word of only one soldier. We've spoken to the other soldiers who were at the site, but they heard nothing. This particular soldier was the sole one interacting with Quessem while the others were watching over the demolition. As you know, we must be very sure about these rumors because there could be fatalities—and I emphasize, fatalities on both sides, Palestinians and Israelis. If these rumors are found to

صداقة يديدوت صداقة يديدوت صداقة يديدوت صداقة يديدوت

صداقة يدىدوت صداقة يدىدوت صداقة يدىدوت صداقة يدىدوت

be unwarranted, then I will release the Quessem family; otherwise, they remain here with us."

"May I be frank with you, Mr. Geller?"

"Go ahead."

"This family said no such thing. I'm sure of it. Of course, he was angry, very angry. His house was being demolished for the only reason that he was too close to the security wall border. How would you feel?"

"Look, Dan, they were given fair warning, enough time to move all their possessions to another home. They were stubborn and wouldn't do it. What were we to do? They gave us no choice. They stood there and deliberately got in the way of the demolition until the soldiers had to bring them in for questioning. They would have gotten killed. Then what?

"There would be headlines all over the papers that the Israeli government is inhumane and killing innocent civilians who refuse to leave their lifelong homes. Wouldn't that make for good public relations around the world for Israel? We are hated no matter what we do, so this would just add to the hatred that people feel for us."

"Aren't you being a bit dramatic? You're part of the machine that keeps churning out all this dissension. These people did nothing except try to save their home, and you accuse them of throwing explosives."

"I'm not the one accusing them. This information was brought to us when the Quessems were brought in here. Let me ask you something. How are you so sure these people are innocent? Do you have a private line into their lives in Tulkarm? Do you know them

صداقة يدىدوت صداقة يدىدوت صداقة يدىدوت صداقة يدىدوت

intimately? You almost have an eerie connection to them in some strange way, and I haven't figured it out yet, but I will."

"And you won't because there isn't any. It's called compassion for a human being, something you left behind a long time ago. How long has it been since you lost your trust and compassion for your fellow man? Maybe long enough to never get it back. Now let me sign those papers and take my children home."

"Whatever you say. Here they are, three of them, sign each at the bottom. … So there is a little fire underneath that quiet exterior," Meshek teased.

Dan was by nature a gentle soul, but Meshek seemed to push him to a level he rarely, if ever, visited. Thinking about what just happened and his reaction to it, Dan felt good about himself and alive for the first time in a long while. He felt a great need to let it go. Dan tended to internalize everything because he always believed if he let any anger show, it would only weaken his spirit, but now he felt differently. He was stronger and more sure of himself. He quickly scanned each document and signed and dated at the bottom and handed the papers back to Meshek, who looked them over.

"Well, everything is in order. Let's say our good-byes to the parents, and you can take your child … children home."

Meshek and Dan went back to the outer office. "Mr. and Mrs. Quessem, please have a few words with your son before he leaves with the Atais."

After a few moments of sobbing, Mrs. Quessem kissed her son. Mr. Quessem hugged Ahmed, assuring him that they would be together soon. Then he walked back toward Dan Atai and stood

صداقة يدىدوت صداقة يدىدوت صداقة يدىدوت صداقة يدىدوت

there staring at him. A tear appeared in his eye, and as he continued to stare at Dan, an almost identical tear appeared in Dan's eye.

Everyone stood by, not daring to break the silence between the two men. Mr. Quessem raised his arms and held them out to hold Dan's hands. They held each other's hands in a tight embrace. Mr. Quessem took a few steps closer. "Thank you, Dan," he whispered into Dan's ears.

Dan whispered back, "I've missed you all these years, my friend."

"Be well," Mr. Quessem said. Words were heard, but the exchange remained unknown to those watching. It was evident that something very special had just taken place.

Meshek shook his head as if to get reassurance that he suspected something more from Dan's outburst in his office, and he was right. He was determined to find out what the connection was between Dan Atai and the Quessem family.

The Quessems were led out of the office by security. Meshek and Abe shook hands with everyone. Meshek looked at Ahmed and said, "Don't get into any more trouble. You are in good hands with this family."

"Yes sir. Thank you."

صداقة يدىدوت صداقة يدىدوت صداقة يدىدوت صداقة يدىدوت

Chapter 8

Dan, Moishe, Joshua, and Ahmed stood outside. Dan called his wife to let her know what was happening. Mrs. Atai couldn't meet them because the gallery was open late. She told Dan she would meet him later at home to find out exactly what had happened. He assured her everything turned out fine, but she needed to know the details. After his phone conversation, they decided to go to the deli to get some dinner.

"Ahmed, you are going to have a different experience tonight. Have you ever eaten pastrami or corned beef?"

"What?" asked Ahmed.

Joshua laughed. "Well, tonight you are, Ahmed. Your belly will be so full, I'll have to roll you around like a soccer ball if you want to turn over in bed."

"I'm not so sure I would like that, Joshua." Ahmed looked skeptical, not sure if he was going to enjoy this Israeli experience. "I trust you though, so I'll continue my adventure."

"Brave, boy." Joshua waved his arm upward, coming down hard with a smack on Ahmed's back.

"Ouch. I don't want to be that brave!"

"Sorry, friend. Let's go."

They arrived at the deli, which was bustling with people inside

صداقة يديدوت صداقة يديدوت صداقة يديدوت صداقة يديدوت

and at the outdoor tables. "Let's get a table outside. It's a beautiful evening," Dan suggested to everyone.

They found a table near the end of the deli and sat down. As they were getting themselves comfortable, a server approached quickly. "Good evening, gentlemen and young sabras. Would you like a beverage to start?"

The server was a beautiful young woman, tall and slender with long, curly golden hair. Her blue eyes seemed to glow like a blue sky on a sunny day. Ahmed stared at her as though he had never seen a woman as beautiful as her. Joshua chuckled to himself as he eyed his friend admiring this young woman.

"Excuse me, Ahmed. Would you like something instead of the beverage?" Joshua poked Ahmed's arm, looking at him with a grin on his face that told everyone what was going on. Ahmed's face turned ashen.

"Uh, what? No, a glass of water would be fine. Maybe a glass of pomegranate juice. Yes, yes, that's what I would like, please." Ahmed turned away and pretended to look at the traffic along the street, hoping this would all disappear.

All the beverage orders were taken. Ahmed squinted his eyes as he looked up the street, then he turned around and looked the other way, and then kept searching with his eyes in every direction.

"Are you okay, Ahmed?" Mr. Atai asked.

"Yes, I think so. I was just wondering why there are soldiers standing on many street corners, including ours."

"They're out there for our security. If anything or anyone looks suspicious to them, they are there to confront the situation or protect us if necessary. This is a way of life for us. You try to get

صداقة يديدوت صداقة يديدوت صداقة يديدوت صداقة يديدوت

used to it, but you never really do. It's a constant reminder that our lives may be in danger every day and at any time."

"Oh, I see. Are you used to it?" The question was directed at the two men.

"I think I can speak for both of us," Ben-Horin replied. "We are not used to it. It just is and so we go on with our lives. You cannot stop living. When you do, then the enemy has won. Does that make sense to you?"

"It does. My Abi told me the same thing, but he believes that the world will change and that in the end, people will do the right thing for each other."

"Do you believe your Abi, Ahmed?"

"I want to, but I'm not so sure, only because I don't see it happening."

Joshua interrupted to change the conversation. "Hey, Ahmed, your girlfriend is on her way back."

"Stop, Joshua. She's just a pretty girl, that's all." "Joshua, can't your friend appreciate the beauty that surrounds us. What, you are such a confident young man that girls don't impress you at all." Mr. Atai laughed. Everything stopped when the young woman asked to take their orders. "Would I be impolite if I did not have your, what was it called?" "Pastrami, corned beef? Joshua offered. "Yes that's it. I think I would like to have the Tabbouleh and pita if that is all right with you Mr. Atai." Ahmed's head dropped hoping that he wouldn't have to order the traditional deli food. "You order whatever you like. You can try them another time, okay?" "Sure." Ahmed raised his head, his eyes crinkled up, with a smile to light up the heavens. The orders were taken and brought out quickly.

صداقة يدِيدوت صداقة يدِيدوت صداقة يدِيدوت صداقة يدِيدوت

As the plates were placed in front of them, each one ate as though they were having a race to the finish. Everyone stared at Ahmed, wanting to ask the question that Joshua asked for all of them. "Well, how do you like Israeli tabbouleh?"

Ahmed laughed. "It's almost as good as my Ommy's—really, really good, I'm happy to say. I'm so hungry that it's going down faster than I can appreciate the flavor of it."

They sat for a while with their bellies full, saying little. There had been a lot of words that day, and it was time for a fasting of speech. What seemed like a long time of silence was broken by Mr. Ben-Horin. "It's been a long day for all of us. I think it's time to go home."

"Agreed," Mr. Atai said and signaled to the boys to begin the walk to the bus.

"Mr. Atai and Mr. Ben-Horin, that was a delicious dinner."

Joshua looked at Ahmed. "And what about me? Didn't you enjoy my charming company?"

"Of course, but you already know that. Why should I have to repeat it over and over for your ego, Joshua?"

"Come boys, let's go. You can debate on the way to the bus."

Walking among the lights of this city was very different for Ahmed. In the area of Tulkarm where he had lived, there were few lights to be seen, except for the lights in his home. Roads were dark, and few people were out. Netanya was different and special; the beach was a magnet for attracting the many tourists to its city. It was still early in the evening, and people were returning home from work, having dinner out, and hurrying to events.

Ahmed thought about his parents and wished to be with them,

صداقة يدِيدوت صداقة يدِيدوت صداقة يدِيدوت صداقة يدِيدوت

صداقة ﻳﺪﻳﺪﻭﺕ صداقة ﻳﺪﻳﺪﻭﺕ صداقة ﻳﺪﻳﺪﻭﺕ صداقة ﻳﺪﻳﺪﻭﺕ

and yet he was grateful for this new experience. In a strange way, the demolition of his home introduced him to a different way of life and new people. The only time he had ever heard anything positive about the Israelis was when his father told him about his friend in Netanya. Ahmed was confused. The Atai family and Mr. Ben-Horin were so friendly to him, not hostile and violent the way Israelis had always been talked about in his community.

The bus was arriving as they got to the stop. "Dan, are you sure you want to take the bus home? I can drive you home, and you won't have to spend time on and off the bus with the crowds."

"You've done enough today. Believe it or not, I enjoy riding the bus. I know, don't say what you're thinking. It will be fun for the boys too. Stay in touch, Moishe, and thanks again for your help today."

"My pleasure Dan." As the crowd walked up to the bus steps, Joshua and Ahmed were next. Dan followed behind them and dropped the coins in the slot. It was crowded and noisy, and there was barely room to stand, but Mr. Atai nudged Ahmed and Joshua toward an opening down the aisle. They all stood together as Mr. Atai waved so long to Mr. Ben-Horin through a barely visible opening in the window.

Ahmed and Joshua enthusiastically followed his lead and waved their hands with the little room they had. The bus seemed to jump off the road after every other stop. Ahmed and Joshua held on to the pole and grabbed each other with their free hand to prevent them both from falling into anyone else near them. The bus screeched to a stop, and people held on to their seats and poles to prevent a domino of people falling onto one another.

صداقة ﻳﺪﻳﺪﻭﺕ صداقة ﻳﺪﻳﺪﻭﺕ صداقة ﻳﺪﻳﺪﻭﺕ صداقة ﻳﺪﻳﺪﻭﺕ

صداقة يدّدوت صداقة يدّدوت صداقة يدّدوت صداقة يدّدوت

As the doors opened, Joshua and Ahmed followed Mr. Atai as he made his way to the pavement. They walked down the street toward the house. Their steps hastily found their way to the front door. The lights were on, and Mr. Atai called out to his wife as he set the key in the lock.

"Shalom, I was worried about all of you. Hello, Ahmed, Joshua. I understand you will be staying with us for a short time, Ahmed. It's nice to have you back with us." Mrs. Atai was as friendly and welcoming as she had been during Ahmed's first visit. He felt at ease.

"Here I am again Mrs. Atai and ready to enjoy your hospitality again."

"Hello, Adiva." Dan Atai kissed his wife on the cheek and squeezed her hand. "It's so good to be home. It's been a very long day—*very long*."

"Hi, Ima."

Mrs. Atai grabbed her son and held him close. "Why don't all of you sit down in the living room and get comfortable. You must be very tired. I'll be in shortly. I have a few things to finish up. And have all of you eaten?"

"Yes, Ima. Aba took us to the deli for Ahmed's first deli meal, but he chickened out and ordered taboulleh and pita."

"I didn't chicken out. The taboulleh was tempting, so I went for it. I'll try your pastrami next time. See, I even remembered its name, ha." Ahmed tried to defend himself but knew he really didn't have to for the Atai family.

صداقة يدّدوت صداقة يدّدوت صداقة يدّدوت صداقة يدّدوت

Chapter 9

Aba sat on the couch while Ahmed and Joshua arranged themselves cross-legged on the Persian carpet. Joshua noticed his father's expression had changed from weariness to seriousness. "What is it, Aba? Is something wrong?"

"No, nothing. I was just thinking. Sometimes that's not a good thing to do. The mind needs to rest just like the body does."

"Hey, Ahmed, want to play dominoes?"

"Not right now. I think your Aba is right. The mind needs to rest for a while. A lot went on today, don't you agree? It seemed like an eternity rolled into one day."

"Okay, I'll just sit and stare at both of you. That should keep me well rested." Joshua's father's eyes were closing, but his body was still not at rest. His legs were twitching and his eyelids straining to open, but he kept folding over and pulling a blanket over his body as a shield. Sitting in the chair moving his body from one corner to the other, comfort seemed a faraway dream.

Mrs. Atai came in and called to Dan. His eyes showed surprise as they opened and stared into the space in front of them. He called out in a voice that could barely be heard, "Adiva?"

"Why don't I get the bed ready so you can turn in early? There's no point in having a battle with your body to stay awake. We'll like you much better when you are well rested."

صداقة يديدوت صداقة يديدوت صداقة يديدوت صداقة يديدوت

"No, I was just taking a quick nap. I still have some unfinished business before the day is over." Joshua and Ahmed looked at each other, each expecting an answer to come from one of them. They shrugged their shoulders and waited. "I hope the unfinished business can be accomplished here at home Dan." Adiva was concerned about Dan. He was not in the best of health and the stress he went through today took a toll on him. She just had to look at his face, his cheeks sagging with folds, the sheen on his face gone and she knew. "Yes, yes it can be done right here where I'm sitting. Just give me a minute to get my thoughts together. Adiva, have a seat. You need to hear what I have to say too." Adiva was feeling apprehensive. "Dan, you're frightening me. What is it? What happened today?" "Adiva darling, I love you. Please believe me that what I'm about to tell you will free our souls. This is something I have kept to myself for too long and it will shed light on so many things. First, let me say to you Joshua, you will learn a valuable lesson from what I'm about to tell you and Ahmed you will understand why your father has taught you about having compassion for all people. I don't want anyone getting emotional okay? Is that clear, all of you?" "Yes Aba, we respect and trust you. Please tell us what's on your mind."

"First I want you to know that it was not always like this between the cities of Tulkarm and Netanya. Palestinians were allowed to travel to Netanya for various reasons without the restrictions that are being enforced now. The checkpoint soldiers became familiar with the families and their faces that traveled back and forth. Now I'm telling you about the working people of the city, not the groups who want to create tension among the citizens.

صداقة يديدوت صداقة يديدوت صداقة يديدوت صداقة يديدوت

صداقة ידידות صداقة ידידות صداقة ידידות صداقة ידידות

As you know Saba had a carpet store which is how I got into the business. He had a good heart and was well-loved by everyone. People traveled to buy carpet from him because they knew he had quality prayer rugs and beautiful carpets for the home and he was fair with his prices. When a customer came in bemoaning their financial situation, Saba couldn't resist a hard luck story and would give the rug on credit. Now Saba was not a pushover. He knew who was telling him a story and who was sincere. Here is the punchline; Saba's customers always paid him on time and not once missed a payment. You might wonder why but it was because Saba treated all people with respect and compassion and they returned it." "But Aba," Joshua interrupted, what does this have to do with today? This is a wonderful story about Saba but I don't understand." "Patience, Joshua. I have to start at the beginning, set the stage so to speak, otherwise what I tell you won't have the impact I want it to have, okay?" "Joshua, let your Abi continue." Ahmed nudged him anxious to hear the rest of the story. Yet he was thinking that this story couldn't have anything to do with him, but his adolescent curiosity couldn't be tamed. If anything it seemed like it was going to be a story unlike anything Joshua had ever heard before. Ahmed sat with his eyes fixed on Mr. Atai getting himself ready to try and piece together the puzzle of this story. Just as Mr. Atai was about to continue, the telephone rang. Mr. Atai rolled his eyes shuffling in his chair. "Adiva, would you please get that so I can continue? He couldn't stop his fidgeting and was clearly annoyed at the phone's rude interruption. *This story had to come out*, he thought. *It's been a secret too long.* He didn't even understand why he had kept it a secret. It was a beautiful story about two families.

صداقة ידידות صداقة ידידות صداقة ידידות صداقة ידידות

صداقة ידידות صداقة ידידות صداقة ידידות صداقة ידידות

There was nothing to hide from anyone, certainly not his family, but he chose to put it at the back of his mind to be forgotten about forever. It was a bittersweet memory that he kept to himself since he was a young boy. He continued to think about it as he heard Adiva's conversation in the background. *Was I that hurt, bruised, wounded as a child that this could not be discussed?* Mr. Atai realized today that fate had the upper hand and demanded he confront his story. There was no turning back now. He had to do this for all the Joshua's and Ahmed's who were out there. Adiva walked back into the living room. "That was Moishe Ben-Horin. He wanted to be sure all of you arrived home safely. I told him yes you were all fine but tired and that you were relaxing. He said he would speak to you tomorrow." "Thank you Adiva. Now I will continue." "Where was, ah yes, your Saba. Anyway, Saba was quite a businessman and human being. It was a very hot summer day when a gentleman and his young son came in. I was a young boy of ten and reluctantly went in to help my Aba, your Saba that day. I guess it was meant for me to be there, on that particular day. I was in the front of the store when they came in and called to Saba that he had a customer. Saba knew immediately that this was not an Israeli Jew and greeted the man and his son with an, "Assalamalakim." The man smiled at both me and Aba and responded with "Shalom."

This was an unusual exchange because of the man greeting Saba with the same respect for his culture. They shook hands and the man introduced himself and his young son. My Aba did the same. Introductions were made between each of the boys and my Aba said the boys could play in the back room while he conducted business. After what seemed like an hour my new friend and I

صداقة ידידות صداقة ידידות صداقة ידידות صداقة ידידות

came out from the back room to find my Aba sipping coffee with this gentleman. They were laughing and smiling at us. I remember Aba saying, "Do you know where my new friend lives?" Of course I didn't and looked at Aba waiting to hear the news. "He lives in the West Bank, in a city called Tulkarm. Isn't that something?" I think I said it sure is or something like that but I didn't know why this news was such a surprise. Let me go on. Joshua interrupted, "This is a very nice story Aba but what does this have to do with anything?" "Joshua, my son, who I raised up to be a genius, please listen and perhaps you can begin to put the pieces together. You too Ahmed, listen carefully and I will continue. "I was just thrilled to have a new friend and during those times we lived among our Arab-Israeli neighbors but this family was different. They were Palestinian and they traveled into Netanya for shopping and for the Aba to sell his fruits and vegetables. We respected one another, did business together and learned about how much we actually had in common. That was until the troublemakers begin to stir things up. Well, I don't want to get off track with my story. This gentleman and his son would stop by weekly to have coffee and conversation with your Saba. In order to do this he entered Netanya at checkpoint for shopping purposes. When my Aba knew they were coming to the store he would take me with him. I was always excited to see my new friend. Don't get me wrong. I had a nice group of boys that I played with and went to school with but this boy was different. I enjoyed having a friendship with a Palestinian though I never said this to my friends. Everyone was not taught tolerance like I was. I would bring my soccer ball and my chess game. We would spend a few hours kicking the ball in the park and

صداقة يديدوت صداقة يديدوت صداقة يديدوت صداقة يديدوت

then come back to play a game of chess. The time passed quickly and I was so disappointed when he had to leave. Aba's customers would come in and interrupt them but the gentleman would wait patiently until Aba completed his transaction and then Aba would continue the conversation. So, has either one of you put any of the pieces together? Mr. Atai waited a moment but wouldn't divulge any information to them. "Aba, can you give us a clue?" Joshua pleaded. "Ha, a clue, everything I told you is a clue." Joshua looked towards his Ima for any expression that might give some clue as to the meaning of this story. Ima remained serious and said nothing. It was clear to Joshua she was on Aba's side on this one. "Hmmn, Ahmed," Joshua whispered, "Do you have ideas about any of this?" "Well, I do have some ideas but I want to hear more to see if I'm right and I'm not telling you. You'll have to wait and try to put it together yourself." "I thought you were my friend?" Joshua taunted. "Don't spoil the fun your Aba is having. Can't you see it on his face? He's enjoying playing with us with this story of his." "You're right Ahmed, as usual." "Boys, please, let's continue. Ahmed won't be with us forever and this may be the only chance I have to cleanse my soul of this secret." Aba stared deeply at both boys, not even a glimmer of a smirk to show some humor. There wasn't any just a man ready to unfold something so deep and important to him. "Sorry Aba. We promise not to interrupt anymore."

"I looked forward to visiting your Saba's shop every week just to see and play with my new friend. Well, the years passed and we were teenagers, perhaps 13 or so, close to your age. We became very close friends and so did our families. We formed a bond even though we were friends from a distance. When he came to the shop

صداقة يديدوت صداقة يديدوت صداقة يديدوت صداقة يديدوت

صداقة ידידות صداقة ידידות صداقة ידידות صداقة ידידות

we resumed our friendship until the visit was over and then it was back to Tulkarm. It was a wonderful time in my life but then …" Aba's voice trailed off to a whisper and then stopped. "But then what Aba, what, please don't stop now. I know something's happened, I do and it doesn't sound good. Please continue." Joshua pleaded. "I'm sorry but I will never get used to the illogical injustices that go on in our world. During those times Arab Israelis and Israelis lived peacefully together, well as peacefully as could be expected and Palestinians had access to Netanya and other cities. Except for the small groups of troublemakers, we all had a decent life and respected one another. Did we love one another? No, it never went that far but we were civil to one another and sociable during our business interactions. Everything started to turn upside down and there was so much strife. The bombing of innocent people began again, rocks were thrown at our soldiers, and the international news couldn't wait to take sides and report these episodes to spread untruths and propaganda, but that's a story for another evening. Before we knew it the people who we lived among as good neighbors now became our enemies. They were looked upon as evil and couldn't be trusted. Every move they made was watched. Every person who walked among us, adults or children, it didn't matter were suspicious. Travel to Netanya by the Palestinians became restrictive, if not impossible. They were given a difficult time at the checkpoints. There were arguments, yelling and threatening by the soldiers and the people. Many were turned away and told to go home. It became so bad because of the troublemakers. "So, what happened Aba, tell us." "There was still traveling back and forth to trade and purchase goods and work but it was never the

صداقة ידידות صداقة ידידות صداقة ידידות صداقة ידידות

صداقة يديدوت صداقة يديدوت صداقة يديدوت صداقة يديدوت

same. You know the checkpoints, documents and such became very strict. Everyone was made to feel guilty, but guilty of what? Now you have the situation with Ahmed and his family. Houses are being torn down for no other reason than they are too close to the wall. It's housing people in one giant prison. I understand the need for security because of all the explosions and deaths they have caused but we are targeting every Palestinian citizen. I just wish the government could find a better way. Anyway, my new, good friend visited the shop one day with his Aba to say goodbye. He told Aba that it was just too much trouble to come to Netanya. I knew why but I still couldn't understand. It was so hard for me to have to end my friendship with such a good and kind friend. We had no choice because the decision had been made for all of us. Of course, not all Israelis were as sad as my Aba and me. Many were glad to see the limited travel and enforced security measures, but we were not one of them. My Aba and Ima taught me to respect everyone and to take the time to know each person I met. Aba always said, "Do not judge a human being based on a group of troublemakers who claim to be of the same cloth." "Aba, please, when are we getting to the punch line of the story? I can't stand it a minute longer." "Oh Joshua, please let me enjoy my storytelling. I'm sure it will be worth the wait." "He knows how to keep his audience in suspense because he wants you to try and figure out what he is leading up to. Listen for his excellent clues." Ima said. Joshua fixed his position and crossed his legs even more and dropped his head down to his arms. Sitting there sulking didn't make him look like an interested audience. Ahmed put his hands on Joshua's shoulders to lift him up. "Now that's better Joshua. I think your Aba is getting to the

صداقة يديدות صداقة يديدות صداقة يديدות صداقة يديدות

best part. Now listen." "Oh sure, like you know. Stop trying to get on my Aba's good side." Joshua pushed Ahmed knocking him down on the rug. Ahmed pushed back. "Boys please. Is this worth fighting over? Use your energy for connecting the pieces."

"Okay, my young men listen carefully. Ahmed is right Joshua. I am getting to the best part of the story but when I do I don't want any dramatics, jumping up and down, or screaming. Is that a deal?" Both boys looked at one another, shrugged and shook their heads. "Of course Aba, whatever you want." Joshua answered with some doubt in his voice. Joshua's enthusiasm was beginning to wane. He just wanted Aba to get to the punchline. It wasn't guaranteed the promise was a solid one. "As I was saying, my friend and I were exchanging our goodbyes and we traded addresses promising to write one another. We vowed our friendship and the bond we created would never be broken, that nothing and no one would ever interfere with the friendship we had forged from that first visit to my Aba's shop. My Aba hugged his friend and I hugged mine. We wished them good health and safety. My Aba decided to close his shop early that day. He and I knew we would never see them again. Even though travel was restricted it certainly wasn't like it is today. This brings me to the strange events that happen in life. Sometimes things happen of which we have no control and yet these situations can be so ironic that I have to wonder if some entity is planning all of this. Does anything I've said this evening sound familiar to both of you? Have you been able to connect any dots? Joshua and Ahmed looked at one another, their eyes squinting tightly to make their brains work harder. They waited for the other to say something but there was silence. Neither one wanted to take

صداقة يديدות صداقة يديدות صداقة يديدות صداقة يديدות

صداقة ידידות صداقة ידידות صداقة ידידות صداقة ידידות

a chance on being wrong but both wanted to be right. Aba was staring at them without blinking. He seemed to want to rush at both of them and shake them into knowing something, anything of what he was trying to say in his story. "All right, I'll just say it. Are you ready" "Oh my goodness Aba, please stop torturing us." Aba took a deep breath and as it settled at the top of his chest sighed. "The man and woman at the station your parents, Ahmed." Aba paused. The silence was making all of them nervous even Ima. Her eyes began searching the room, searching for a place to focus her stare. Ahmed jumped out involuntarily, "Mr. Atai, no, no it can't be, is it, are they, is he?" "Ahmed, what are you trying to say? Aba, what are you trying to tell us?" Joshua yelled. "Joshua, if it's what I'm thinking, my father was the boy in the story." "And?" Joshua still hadn't figured it out. "Joshua, don't you see, my father was the boy who became friends with your Aba, isn't that right Mr. Atai? I guessed it, didn't I? didn't I?" "That's not it? Yes, it has to be." Ahmed looked at Mr. Atai for reassurance. Mr. Atai said nothing and got up from his chair. He calmly walked over to Joshua and Ahmed. Mrs. Atai walked over to meet them. She had tears in her eyes for she knew Ahmed was right. Mr. Atai put his arms around both boys. "Yes, Ahmed. You are right. Your Aba was and will always be my good friend. When we saw one another, we couldn't believe it. It was a miracle that we were brought together again under such conditions. We had to be strong because of the delicate situation for all of you. It was not going to be a happy reunion. We didn't want the officials to be suspect of anything so we embraced in a friendly way from one Aba to another. Another person would have been hysterical, shouting at me, the officials, whoever, but

صداقة ידידות صداقة ידידות صداقة ידידות صداقة ידידות

صداقة ﻳﺪﻳﺪوت صداقة ﻳﺪﻳﺪوت صداقة ﻳﺪﻳﺪوت صداقة ﻳﺪﻳﺪوت

your Aba knew you were in good hands with me and my family. There was one problem, however, and that was the official, Meshek. He suspected something between us but he wasn't sure what and he knew I would say nothing to him. I know people pretty well and I'm sure he's trying to figure out the connection. I could see from the corner of my eye that he was trying to hear what your Aba and I were saying to one another. His sleuthing skills were failing him at that moment and he was frustrated but he knew better than to try and push me into saying something. Ha, I don't think I've heard the last of Meshek. Ahmed and Joshua looked hypnotized as they listened to Mr. Atai's story. Finally, Ahmed could no longer remain silent. "Mr. Atai, you must have felt the way Joshua and I feel right now, that we must say our goodbyes and pretend our friendship never existed." "Yes, Ahmed, it was something like that, but time and growing up has a way of helping us to forget those past times. Also, your Aba and I promised to never break the bond of our friendship. Of course, in our hearts I think we knew it was a breakable bond, out of our control. That's what happened to me; I grew up, went into the Israeli Army, met my wife, got married, had children and took over my father's shop. I made new friends and got to meet a lot of people. Time did erase a lot of the memories except one, your Aba. It's very difficult to abandon a close friendship one has as a child. I think my friendship with your Aba was so special because it helped to fuel my compassion for people, and it helped me to understand the bad ones and how they can manipulate entire communities to hate to serve their purpose. Our experiences when we are young, Ahmed, randomly help to shape the people we become. You might not realize it now,

صداقة ﻳﺪﻳﺪوت صداقة ﻳﺪﻳﺪوت صداقة ﻳﺪﻳﺪوت صداقة ﻳﺪﻳﺪوت

صداقة يديدوت صداقة يديدوت صداقة يديدوت صداقة يديدوت

but there are people who will affect your life in ways you will not know until much later on. Do you understand what I'm trying to tell you, Ahmed?" "Yes, I do, Mr. Atai, but what if there are people who affect us in a negative way, and those people outweigh the good experiences we have, then what? Don't you think that's what has happened to all the troublemakers who want to destroy the kind of friendship that Joshua and I have? Weren't they the people who destroyed the friendship between you and my Abi?" "You are partially right, Ahmed. You must remember that for all the troublemakers there are the people who are working for peace and goodwill among us. Please keep that in your mind when you encounter the troublemakers, okay?" "I'll try Mr. Atai." Ahmed promised. "Aba," Joshua interrupted, "now that you have seen Mr. Qussem after all these years how do you feel about it? You know you won't be able to see him again once they bring Ahmed and his family back to Tulkarm." "Joshua, life will go on as it always has and I will pray that my friend is able to live a peaceful existence with his family. That's all I can say, there's nothing else I have the power to do." Joshua walked over to his Aba and put his arms around him, hugging him with all the strength he had. "I love you Aba. You are a good man." Joshua's words were filled with tears. Mrs. Atai quickly embraced both and put her arm out for Ahmed to join them. Joshua and Mr. Atai loosened their hold and wrapped their arms around Mrs. Atai and Ahmed forming a circle of hugs. "Well, this has been quite an eventful and emotional day. We will sleep well tonight knowing that your parents and you are safe." "Mr. Atai, do you think they will release my parents tomorrow so that we can return to Tulkarm?" "I'm sure they will. Your parents

صداقة يديدوت صداقة يديدوت صداقة يديدوت صداقة يديدوت

have done nothing wrong, nothing illegal, except maybe yelling a little too loudly at the soldiers. They're a sensitive bunch and they have to be very careful or it can cost them their lives. You understand, Ahmed, it was nothing personal. That is how they are trained. Meshek will call me tomorrow. I'm just not sure when. Get ready for bed and don't worry about anything. It will work out. You have my word, Ahmed." "I know Mr. Atai. You make me feel better. Come Joshua, let's go to your room and talk a little before bed, okay?" "Sounds good, Ahmed. Good night Aba, Ima." "Good night, Mr. and Mrs. Atai and thank you for everything, for what you've done for me and for my family." Ahmed's words were cracking so he turned around quickly before the tears he began to feel would be streaming down his face. "Come on Joshua." "I'm way ahead of you Ahmed." Joshua teased as he ran down the hall to his room.

Chapter 10

Joshua turned the light on as Ahmed followed behind. "You wash up first Ahmed. I'll get things ready for us." "Okay Joshua but don't do anything sneaky. I've had enough excitement for one day." Joshua could hear the water running in the bathroom and walked down the hall back to the living room where his Aba sat quietly. "Aba, may I speak to you for one moment before Ahmed and I go to sleep?" "Of course, Joshua, what is it? You seem concerned. Is everything all right?" "Well, I was just thinking. What if the authorities don't release Ahmed's parents? Then what will happen? Do you think they know where his sister and Saba are? Do you think they will bring Ahmed back to Tulkarm and his family? "Joshua, in this case, I believe they will do what is right and what is fair. Our security people have all the information on the Quessem family. They know where Ahmed's Saba and sister are living. Believe me they have every piece of information they could gather. Fairness doesn't always happen of course, but this is not the usual situation that they encounter. I don't want you to go to bed worrying about this, do you understand?" Joshua hesitated. "Do you believe me Joshua?" "I've always believed you Aba. It's everyone else that I question." "Good and you should. There's nothing wrong with questioning. That's how you learn. Okay, now go to bed and don't worry about Ahmed. I'm sure he has a lot on his mind with concern

صداقة يديدوت صداقة يديدوت صداقة يديدوت صداقة يديدوت

for his family." "He does Aba, good night." "Good night Joshua, sleep well." "Done," Ahmed said. Now it's your turn. I'm crashing Joshua, just too tired to do anything else, okay?" "Sure. See you in the morning." Ahmed nestled his head into the pillow dreaming about being with his family again. He smiled at the thought of it and drifted off to sleep.

As the light came streaming in through the opening in the shade, Joshua felt a heavy tugging on his arm. He thought he was dreaming and pulled away turning his body away from the sun. "Joshua, wake up, it's Ahmed. Come on, it's morning, wake up, please." Ahmed kept pulling at Joshua who finally opened his eyes. "What's going on, why are you awake? Do we have to be somewhere?" "I'm sorry Joshua. I couldn't sleep and just wanted some company. It was not a good night for me. Getting to sleep was easy because I had good feelings about being home with my family. Then in my deepest sleep I had nightmares that I wouldn't see my parents ever again." "Stop thinking that way. My Aba would never let that happen. Please believe me. He said this is a different situation, not the usual "outsider" trying to make trouble." Joshua yawned and stretched but was having difficulty being fully awake. He finally sat up and stared at Ahmed. "Would you feel differently? Would you be so calm and cool that you say I should be if it were your parents? Be honest Joshua. Don't tell me fairy tales. I want the truth." There was an uncomfortable silence as each boy stared down the other. "Well Joshua, what's your answer? Or do you have one that I will believe?" "Do you see I'm thinking Ahmed?" Joshua asked. "I have to choose my words before I speak. Now give me a minute." "Joshua, this is a serious situation that I can't take

صداقة يديدوت صداقة يديدوت صداقة يديدوت صداقة يديدوت

lightly. I'm sorry for sounding like I'm blaming you, I'm not, but I'm really worried." "Listen Ahmed, think about it. The authorities let you come home with me instead of keeping you there with your parents. They could have easily done that and then told my parents and I to go home and forget about the whole situation, but they didn't did they? My father is trustworthy and they wouldn't have done that with just anyone." Ahmed's back was to Joshua as he spoke encouraging words to him. Ahmed turned around in deep thought. He remained silent and just stood there looking at Joshua. "You don't believe me, do you Ahmed? I am being as honest as I can right now. Do I have the answers? No, I don't, so I'm giving you my thoughts about what I think happened. The authorities are tough, they don't bend easily and trust no one. They know my Aba wouldn't do anything devious. The only thing he would do is keep you overnight until he hears from them that's all. I have nothing more I can say to convince you. Either you believe and have faith in my words or you don't. Now let's get some breakfast." "I apologize. I do understand what you're telling me but they're still my family and I want to be with them and go back to Tulkarm. I'm just afraid they will send me back and keep them here as prisoners. They've done nothing wrong except to express their feelings about their family home." As Joshua was about to respond, Ima came to the door. "It's time for a good breakfast. I think you two are going to have a very busy day." "Okay, Ima, we'll be a moment." "Listen Ahmed, whether you believe me or not, I know your feelings are real and sincere. Please keep hope in your heart today and think positively about how this will turn out. I will do the same." Ahmed seemed reluctant to respond. As they walked towards the kitchen,

صداقة يديدوت صداقة يديدوت صداقة يديدوت صداقة يديدوت

صداقة يديدوت صداقة يدِيدوت صداقة يدِيدوت صداقة يدِيدوت

Ahmed put his arm around Joshua. "You've been a good friend to me, Joshua. There is no hatred in my heart for you and your family, only love. Would you let your Ima know that I want to say my morning prayers before I sit down to breakfast?" "Of course I will. Go ahead and I'll see you when you have finished your prayers."

As Ahmed lay on his knees on the carpet that Mr. Atai had given him, he began his morning prayers, but was startled by the phone ringing. It took what seemed like forever for someone to answer it. He could faintly hear Mrs. Atai's conversation and felt guilty about stopping his prayers to eavesdrop. "Yes, one moment please, I'll go get him. ... Daniel, there is a phone call for you from Meshek Geller."

"Thanks Adiva. Please tell him I'll be right there." Dan was surprised at being called Daniel. It was a long time since his wife had addressed him that way, and he felt a little unsettled. He thought something was wrong, and Ahmed quickly came into his thoughts.

"He'll pick up in a moment," Mrs. Atai assured Meshek.

"Shalom, how are you? ... Yes, really? Are you sure? ... What caused such a change of heart? This is unlike our security people to be so bold. I'm sorry, but you can appreciate that this is quite unexpected." Mrs. Atai stood by, fascinated by what she was hearing. She was trying to put the pieces together but she needed to hear more.

"Well, I certainly appreciate your sense of humanity in this situation. It means a great deal to me and my friendship with the boy's father. It's been so many years, and it's hard to forget such a friendship made when you're a young boy.

صداقة يدِيدوت صداقة يدِيدوت صداقة يدِيدوت صداقة يدِيدوت

صداقة ﻳﺪﻳﺪﻭﺕ صداقة ﻳﺪﻳﺪﻭﺕ صداقة ﻳﺪﻳﺪﻭﺕ صداقة ﻳﺪﻳﺪﻭﺕ

"I understand your responsibilities, and I will follow your instructions to the letter. Don't worry. I realize you are putting yourself out for me, very unusual to say the least. Again, I am grateful to you. What time will you be coming by with them, and when will they be taken back to Tulkarm?"

Mr. Atai wanted to be sure he didn't say anything that could change this generous favor that he was about to experience. "Of course, everything will be documented for me to follow when you get here? Good, very good, and thank you again. I look forward to seeing them." Mr. Atai turned around, holding the phone in midair and staring at his wife.

Ahmed had finished his prayers but felt uncomfortable coming into the room at that moment, so he stayed where he was until the conversation was finished. Joshua approached him with his arms raised up. "What's going on?"

"Sshh … I heard a conversation between your Aba and I'm sure someone from the station, but I don't know what it's about. Your father was about to tell your mother what's going on. Let's stay here and try to listen to what's being said."

"Wow, it sounds like some foreign intrigue to me, Ahmed."

"Stop your joking; this could be serious and could concern me and my parents."

"Sorry."

From the other room, the boys could just make out the conversation. "Adiva, you won't believe what just happened."

"No, I guess I won't if you don't tell me. Please, what was that all about? I know who called you, remember?"

"Oh, of course you do. Well, Meshek had a conversation with

Quessem, and he told him of our friendship when we were young boys. He explained to him what a shock it was to see me and to find out that my son had befriended Ahmed. He went on to tell Meshek how life has a way of planning for us without having to ask. It seems this story was sincere enough for Meshek that he arranged for the family to come here and stay with us until evening. Then they will come and take all of them back to Tulkarm.

"After the investigation, they found that Quessem was just being passionately argumentative with the soldiers and nothing more. That he was not going to do harm to anyone, and all he wanted was for his home to be left alone. This move is very uncharacteristic of the security, but they wouldn't have agreed to this unless they were sure these people were not Hamas or another group like them.

"There are rules we will follow as to the time and the pickup, but I assured Meshek that we would follow it every step of the way. So, what do you think?"

"You may not want to hear this, but I feel I must say it anyway. I'm suspicious of why they're showing such compassion in this particular situation. I just don't want any harm to come to the Quessem family and certainly not to us. Am I being too distrustful, Dan?"

"No not at all. This is our country and what we have become accustomed to in our life. It's fine to question their motives. After all, this is not a daily happening here. It is just a very different protocol so you are wise to question it. I feel good about it and think that something got through to Meshek and after careful consideration, he and his staff decided it would be safe to do this. I do believe they will have several soldiers stationed outside the

صداقة يديدوت صداقة يديدوت صداقة يديدوت صداقة يديدوت

house. They're not that trusting." Dan winked at his wife, knowing she understood exactly what he meant.

"I agree with you, and for whatever reason, I'm grateful that you will be able to see Quessem again in our home in a more relaxed and social environment. I'll call the children for breakfast, and you'll let them know what's going on."

"Excellent. You are a good wife and someone I can always count on." Dan walked toward her, put his hands on her shoulders, and sweetly kissed her forehead. Mrs. Atai began to pull back from surprise, but returned his kiss with another as she embraced him. His arms surrounded her body as they enjoyed this moment of tenderness.

Suddenly Joshua walked into the room. "Sorry, Aba and Ima, for interrupting." He looked embarrassed by his parents' affection.

"Come here, Joshua. You can share in this too." Both Aba and Ima wrapped their arms around their only surviving son. Tears began to appear in their eyes, and Ima quickly moved away.

"Come, let's eat a good breakfast now. We have a big day ahead of us. Joshua, please get Ahmed." Ima's tone suddenly turned authoritative as she said this.

"Yes, Ima." Joshua obeyed. He knew how much Ima and his Aba had suffered when Avram was killed. He kept this in mind whenever his parents showed anger or sadness directed at him, and he forgave them. He understood. Avram's death forced him to accept this loss and made him more sensitive to his parents' behavior and moods.

صداقة يديدوت صداقة يديدوت صداقة يديدوت صداقة يديدوت

Chapter 11

Joshua quietly walked toward his room, careful not to disturb Ahmed from his prayers. He found Ahmed sitting on the bed. "Did you complete your prayers? Ima says it's time for breakfast."

"Yes. I'm hungry, are you? Prayers always give me an appetite." Ahmed chuckled and broke the moment's seriousness. Joshua laughed along with him. "Then let's not waste another minute or Aba will eat it all!"

Joshua and Ahmed walked to the kitchen and found Aba and Ima already at the table. Ahmed couldn't help but stare at Aba's hand resting on Ima's. He thought how sweet it was to see two parents so affectionate with one another. He wished he was looking at his own parents. He missed the scenes of his Ommy preparing the morning meal and the smell of strong coffee brewing before the family knelt for morning prayers. It will happen again. He tried to think positively, knowing that the family he was with had helped him and his family during this stressful time.

"Well, good morning my young men, and how are we on this fine morning?" Aba seemed in an especially joyful mood, unlike any other that Ahmed had witnessed. Even Joshua was delighted at his Aba's playfulness.

"Come and sit down. Ima has made a special breakfast because we have such good news to tell you."

صداقة يديدوت صداقة يديدوت صداقة يديدوت صداقة يديدوت

Ahmed and Joshua stared at each other puzzled. *What good news could Aba possibly have to tell us that changed from last night to now?* Joshua tried to find something that he could connect to yesterday's events and couldn't.

Ahmed remembered the phone call that morning while he had begun his prayers. He wished he could have heard what the conversation was about, but it was too difficult, so he had gone back to complete his prayers. *The news has to be about that conversation because nothing else has changed,* Ahmed thought. His mind was racing faster than ever as one thought after another about his parents kept filtering into his mind.

They sat down at the table to hear what Aba had to say. Ahmed and Joshua looked at Aba, waiting, but nothing was forthcoming. "Okay, Aba, what is this news you want to tell us?"

"Patience, my son, I'm waiting for Ima to bring breakfast so she can sit down with us, right Ima?" Aba asked.

"Of course, this is very special news indeed, and I want to be part of the conversation." Now Ahmed and Joshua began squirming in their chairs, impatient at having to wait to hear the news. Ima walked over with plates of food. "Go ahead, Dan, don't keep them in suspense any longer like you did last night."

"I agree, you win this time. Well, we have all been blessed, and I can't explain to you why, but we should be appreciative of the good nature of Meshek Geller. Ahmed, he is allowing your parents to visit with us the entire day. Then all of you will be picked up and driven back to Tulkarm in the evening."

"What? With all respect to you, Mr. Atai, I cannot believe this. This doesn't sound right to me. Something is going on. Do

صداقة يديدوت صداقة يديدوت صداقة يديدوت صداقة يديدوت

you trust his word? I don't. He seems like a sneaky man." Ahmed was surprised and distrustful.

"It is all true, and I was as surprised as you are right now. Mrs. Atai felt the same way you do. She asked me what plan Mr. Geller had. I assured her as I'm assuring you right now that your Abi had been convinced by him to explain the look we exchanged at our meeting. I sensed that he suspected something, but I let it go. Obviously he didn't. He's a smart one that Meshek Geller. He got your Abi to tell him the whole story."

"Wow, Mr. Atai, all of this has been so strange. I didn't like him and didn't trust him when I was taken to the station. He was really mean to me and made me feel like I was a criminal before even asking my name. I guess there's a soft spot somewhere inside of him." Ahmed laughed, and so did the rest of the Atai family.

Joshua let his Aba and Ahmed do all the talking. After all, this was about Ahmed and his family. Joshua was there to lend support to his friend when he needed it, and he was enjoying the exchange between both of them.

"Ahmed, sometimes we are too quick to make judgments of people based on our past experiences, but once in a while, we are jolted by the unexpected kindness shown to us by people we perceive as our enemy." Mr. Atai knew how quickly Ahmed would judge any Israeli who showed negativity toward him. He was grateful that Meshek was able to show another facet of his gruff personality.

"So let's eat breakfast and get ready for your parents' arrival at noon. Our good Ima has fixed a splendid breakfast for us. I will say our prayer before we eat, and you may do the same, Ahmed."

Ahmed was going to miss the hospitality and good nature of

صداقة يديدوت صداقة يديدوت صداقة يديدوت صداقة يديدوت

صداقة يديدوت صداقة يديدوت صداقة يديدوت صداقة يديدوت

the Atai family. He understood so clearly how his Abi and Mr. Atai became friends. In many ways, they were very much alike.

The more Ahmed thought about it, the more he realized that his Abi and Mr. Atai and he and Joshua seemed related. They looked so much alike, and his Abi and Mr. Atai always spoke of the goodness of human beings and not to think that all people outside their community were evil.

Ahmed was feeling very happy. He thought about being with his parents again and how much he had missed them. It was going to be good to be a family again even if they weren't living in their home. He knew that eventually his Abi would find another home to live in. Did his parents know where they would be going upon returning to Tulkarm? Yes, of course they knew. Ahmed reassured himself, erasing any doubt he may have started feeling.

Ahmed said a prayer and waited for Mr. Atai and the family to finish their prayer. He waited until they took their first forkful of food and then he quickly picked up a forkful that he could barely fit into his mouth. Ahmed's Ability to retrieve food and empty it into his mouth while barely coming up for air was an incredible sight.

Joshua looked up from his plate and saw the speed with which Ahmed was eating. "Hey, Ahmed, slow down. Your parents won't be here until noon." Mr. and Mrs. Atai smiled at Ahmed. They understood the anxiety he must have been feeling about being reunited with his parents.

"It's all right," Mrs. Atai interrupted. "You eat as fast as you'd like. This is a special day for you and for us too. Your parents' visit will give Mr. Atai a chance to reminisce with your Abi, and I can

صداقة يديدوت صداقة يديدوت صداقة يديدوت صداقة يديدوت

get to know your Ommy. Is there anything I can make for them? I would love to try and prepare something special."

"Mrs. Atai, maybe you and my Ommy can make something together. That would be meaningful for both of you, wouldn't it?"

"Of course it would. What a wonderful idea. Why don't you let me know a dish that you love for dinner, and I will get the ingredients so Ommy and I can prepare it together, okay?"

"That sounds great. Do you have a pen and paper, and I'll write down all the ingredients you'll need."

"This is exciting. I'm looking forward to your parents' visit. Finish eating, everyone, and then Ahmed, you'll give me the ingredients." Ahmed was hungry, quickly spooning the eggs into his mouth, followed by a large bite of bread. He seemed to be dancing in his seat with each forkful because he was so excited at the prospect of seeing his parents. *This will be a great party,* he thought. *It will be unforgettable.*

As he thought about it more, he realized it would be bittersweet because his friendship with Joshua and the Atais was coming to an end. Why did it have to? *Why can't we continue to be friends and see one another?* It didn't seem fair, and he knew it was never fair when it came to the Israeli and Palestinian people. *Why do we have to be punished because of those who hate and want power?*

"Ahmed, there you go again, in deep thought and finished with breakfast too," Joshua joked.

"I'll go get the paper and pen, and you can write down everything. Please tell me anything you think you and your parents would enjoy."

"Yes, Mrs. Atai, of course I will." There was a sadness Mrs. Atai

صداقة يديدות صداقة يديدות صداقة يديدות صداقة يديدות

detected in Ahmed's voice, and she had several reasons for it, but she knew there was nothing she could do to change the situation.

She, like Ahmed, also knew the cruelty in which innocent people pay the price for those who cause trouble. She had lived with it all her life. Mrs. Atai was experiencing many of the same emotions as Ahmed when she thought about the reunion of her husband and Mr. Quessem. It would be one filled with both joy and sadness.

Enough of these morbid thoughts, she said to herself. *It's time to rejoice and have a celebration! This is a wonderful moment for my family and Ahmed's.* "I'm ready when you are. Go ahead," Mrs. Atai said enthusiastically.

"Mrs. Atai, what I am about to say is with all respect to you, but I want to tell you what a traditional meal would be like in my home."

"By all means, Ahmed, please be honest. I want this to be a memorable day."

"Okay, first you should put out a platter of olives. Of course, they should be a plate of different kinds of olives, then a wonderful Arabic salad with a main meal of kafta hamra. Ooh, even full with breakfast, I'm making myself hungry already." Mrs. Atai and Ahmed shared a great laugh.

"Go on, Ahmed. This sounds wonderful."

"And for dessert, some dates, figs, and nuts, and a beautiful sponge cake. How's that?"

"You should be a chef. You have a good appreciation for the foods you eat."

"My Ommy always said I was the reason she enjoyed cooking

Mrs. Atai. I'll write down the ingredients and you can choose which ones you will make."

"I like that, but I will make everything. You give me the ingredients, and I will go to the market and pick up what I need to start preparing. Oh this will be the best day!" Mrs. Atai couldn't hold back her excitement. She was a woman who was used to social events, especially with the art gallery. This, however, was very different than sharing a glass of wine with a new artist and their audience. The Quessems' visit was something she would experience once in a lifetime.

Joshua sat silently by while the exchange between Ahmed and his mother was completed. "Now, Ahmed, finish up your recipes so we can play a little ball. Hey, you know what? I have some new shorts and a T-shirt you can wear today. I think Ima has washed your clothes enough. Aren't you tired of wearing the same things for the past two days?"

"Stop it, Joshua. I'm fine, but since you are offering some new clothes, I certainly won't turn you down. I'll wear them after we play and I shower before my parents' visit. Now let me finish this for your Ima, and we'll go."

"Whatever you say, Ahmed. It's your day."

"That's it. I'm finished." Ahmed walked down the long hallway to the kitchen. Mrs. Atai was finishing the breakfast dishes and turned around to see Ahmed. She smiled sweetly at him, and he thought Mrs. Atai was such a beautiful, loving mother. At that moment Ahmed felt close to her and wanted to run up and embrace her for being a second mother to him, but he hesitated. He didn't

صداقة ידידות صداقة ידידות صداقة ידידות صداقة ידידות

want to make her uncomfortable, and he certainly didn't want to look foolish.

"Here are the recipes, Mrs. Atai." Ahmed proudly held out several pieces of paper filled from top to bottom with his beloved mother's dishes.

"Great and now I'll head out to the market for time is getting close to their arrival. They should be here close to noon. Joshua, I'm leaving now. Please clean up your room; we are having company. Shalom."

Before Joshua could answer, his Ima was out the door. "My Ima is so excited, Ahmed. I haven't seen her like this since the last big opening at her gallery. Your parents are so special to my Aba and Ima. I want you to know how special my friendship has been with you even though it has been a short one."

"Why are you saying it's a short friendship? Is it over, Joshua?" Ahmed looked annoyed, almost angry as he stared intently at Joshua.

"Of course it's not over, but come on, let's be realistic. How are we going to maintain a friendship with you in Tulkarm and me here in Netanya? If you can answer that one, then you truly are some kind of friend."

"Stop goading me, Joshua. You want me to get angry, don't you? You want to see how far you can push me, how violent I can get? Is that it? Is that what you want?" Ahmed took several steps closer to Joshua, glaring at him as he said these words. It was a look Joshua had not seen since he had met Ahmed, and it gave him a scare, though he didn't show it to Ahmed.

"Ahmed, back off. I didn't mean anything other than how will

صداقة يديدوت صداقة يديدوت صداقة يديدوت صداقة يديدوت

we maintain our friendship? Don't you think I want to? If I didn't, I wouldn't have brought you to my home in the first place, and I would have been playing with my friends, but instead I chose to be with you and help you. I didn't care one bit about my friends these past few days. You have no right to accuse me of anything since everything I have done has been with good intentions."

Ahmed stood silent, almost nose to nose with Joshua. He coughed and stepped several steps back to put some space between him and Joshua. "I'm, I'm sorry, but I'm confused, angry, and frustrated. All the Israelis are not like you and your family. One day I have a new friend, and the next we'll be towns apart, but not just in physical miles. We will be separated by our culture, religion, and government. Those things will be responsible for weakening our friendship, don't you see that? We will have no control over that no matter how much we try to keep our friendship together.

"Look what happened with my Abi and your Aba. They were close friends, and then because the government said so, were separated forever. A friendship ended not by anything they did but by outsiders. What kind of crazy world are we living in when people can't like who they want to like? The same will happen to us. It doesn't matter what we want, Joshua.

"We could tell our government about the wonderful friendship we have, the bond we have formed and how we have helped and look out for each other's safety. Do you really think they would care one bit? Ha! Never. I doubt they would even give us a chance to explain our friendship. We'd be arrested for it. That's the crazy world we live in. As far as they're concerned, we should hate one another.

صداقة يديدوت صداقة يديدوت صداقة يديدوت صداقة يديدوت

صداقة يديدوت صداقة يديدوت صداقة يديدوت صداقة يديدوت

That's why it is strange to me that Mr. Meshek was generous in allowing my parents to visit."

Joshua understood every word that Ahmed said, but he wanted to believe so badly that they would prove everyone wrong, that their bond would survive all the hatred and negativity. They would be the example for everyone else to follow. This was Joshua's dream, and he knew that Ahmed shared the same dream—he just wanted to maintain his strong shield of armor in front of Joshua. Joshua knew better, and he also knew that what Ahmed said was true. They would try to keep their friendship alive, but it would be very difficult with the outside forces separating them.

"Ahmed, enough of this talk. Let's play some ball. Before you know it, your parents will be here, and Ima will be preparing a feast for us. ... Aba, Ahmed and I are going to play some ball. We'll be in the courtyard."

"Okay, but don't go too far. The soldiers will be bringing the Quessems here in a few hours."

"Yes, Aba, promise. We'll be close by if you need us." Joshua smiled at Aba. He didn't think there was anything he could do to anger him today. Aba was looking forward to being reunited with his childhood friend, and that's all he had on his mind.

صداقة يديدوت صداقة يديدوت صداقة يديدوت صداقة يديدوت

Chapter 12

"Good morning, Mr. Quessem, Mrs. Quessem," Mr. Meshek greeted them. "I hope you had a restful night and that you have eaten."

"Yes, but it would be more enjoyable in our own home, if I may respectfully say so," Mr. Quessem replied.

"I understand, but I have some news that might make you feel a little better. We are bringing you to the Atais' home today so that you and Dan can spend some time getting reacquainted. We will then pick you up in the evening, and you will be driven back to Tulkarm."

Mr. Quessem stared at Mr. Meshek without saying a word. "What are you thinking, Mr. Quessem? Is this good news for you?" The silence went on, and Mr. Quessem didn't blink. Mrs. Quessem held on to her husband's arm, looking at him and waiting to see what he was going to say or do.

Mr. Quessem seemed to shake himself out of a trance and spoke. Instead of being elated about the visit, he said, "I am grateful to see my childhood friend, but why are you doing this for us?"

"Can't a man do a good deed once in a while? I do know what it means to have a good friend and then to lose him. Fortunately, you have an opportunity to see Dan. I will never see my friend again. I can only think about my friendship with him and the happy

صداقة يديدوت صداقة يديدوت صداقة يديدوت صداقة يديدوت

memories, but you have a chance to briefly relive your memories together. Now does my gesture make sense to you, Mr. Quessem?"

Meshek was insulted that the opportunity he presented was met with distrust, although he was thinking that he shouldn't be surprised. This was a very unusual situation. Normally he wouldn't have gone out of his way to make a visit like this happen as he had done with the Quessems and Atais.

Maybe he was getting older and mellowing, he thought. But it was more than that. Something about these two men touched his emotions in a way that was long hidden inside of him. He was thankful for what happened and that there was an awakening in him that he had suppressed for so many years. As a young man, Meshek had been hardened by the many atrocities he witnessed when he was in the Israeli army and then as a security person in Netanya. He had seen too much and packed away his feelings so that he could continue with his job. If he hadn't, he might not still be alive today. He had been affected by what he had seen to the extent that he spent several years in counseling to help him cope.

Meshek felt he had a great responsibility to keep his people and community safe, and he wouldn't walk away from his job, so he developed a tough, no-nonsense exterior to present to the world, especially those who would bring harm to Israelis.

Mr. Quessem carefully and nervously held out his hand to Mr. Meshek. His dark, moonlike eyes stayed fixed on Meshek's face. "This visit that you have arranged means a lot to me. I haven't seen Daniel since we were teenagers, and it will be wonderful to visit with him as an adult. I will ask no questions and accept your graciousness in arranging this reunion for me and my good friend."

صداقة يديدوت صداقة يديدوت صداقة يديدوت صداقة يديدوت

صداقة ﯾﺪﯾﺪﻭﺕ صداقة ﯾﺪﯾﺪﻭﺕ صداقة ﯾﺪﯾﺪﻭﺕ صداقة ﯾﺪﯾﺪﻭﺕ

"Good. Then it's done. After your prayers, we will leave for the Atais."

"There is one thing, however, Mr. Meshek."

"Yes, what is it?" Meshek looked confused because he thought everything was now in place.

"You say you'll be taking us back to Tulkarm in the evening, but where will you be taking us?"

Mrs. Quessem tugged on her husband's arm. "Remember, I had arranged for an apartment with Mr. Moussa before our home was …" Her voice trailed off. She didn't want to stir up anger in her husband. He had too much to bear, and she was very aware of his feelings. "They can take us there."

"My good wife, how did you know what was going to happen, and when did you take it upon yourself to get a place to live without speaking to me about it?" Mr. Quessem's question was a very serious one, and Meshek could feel the tension between them.

"Now, now, Mr. Quessem. This is what wives are for—thinking ahead and planning for it. I don't mean to intrude, but she is a smart woman, and you are a fortunate man."

"All right. We'll go to the apartment, but remember this: I will be building another home for my family. This is temporary and nothing more."

"Of course it is. That's all it was ever meant to be—just a place to live for the time being." Mrs. Quessem knew how to calm her husband down. There was nothing more important to him than his family, and he needed to know that he could provide for them and protect them.

"Is this where my father and daughter are right now?"

صداقة ﯾﺪﯾﺪﻭﺕ صداقة ﯾﺪﯾﺪﻭﺕ صداقة ﯾﺪﯾﺪﻭﺕ صداقة ﯾﺪﯾﺪﻭﺕ

صداقة يديدوت صداقة يديدوت صداقة يديدوت صداقة يديدوت

"Yes, they will be there when we arrive. That's where I told them to go before we were brought here, so don't worry about them."

Mr. Meshek interrupted the domestic exchange. "Excuse me. As I said, we will be here for you after your prayers at noon. Please be ready to go."

"We will Mr. Meshek." Mr. Quessem then turned around to continue the conversation with his wife.

Meshek shook his head and mumbled as he walked out of their room. As he walked toward his office, he felt someone grab him by the shoulders. Not knowing who it was, he quickly turned around with his arms raised, ready to swing. When he saw Mr. Glaser, his supervisor and the head of the security office, he looked at his fists in front of him and began to squirm.

"A little nervous, Meshek? Sorry to come up behind you like that. I thought you heard my footsteps, but I guess you were in another world, which brings me to my purpose in coming to see you. Let's move into your office, shall we?"

Meshek hesitated for a short moment. "Of course, let's go. Is this something you need to speak to me about in private?"

"Let's just say it's sensitive information and leave it at that."

By the time the conversation ended, they were at the door to Meshek's office. He unlocked the door and moved away to let Mr. Glaser go in first. "Have a seat, please. Would you like some coffee, tea, water?" Meshek offered these beverages as a way to put off what was coming next. He was uncomfortable and had a feeling he wasn't going to like what Mr. Glaser had to say.

"Meshek, you're a good man and a trustworthy one. You have

صداقة يديدوت صداقة يديدوت صداقة يديدوت صداقة يديدوت

صداقة يدىدوت صداقة يدىدوت صداقة يدىدوت صداقة يدىدوت

served us well and have been conscientious in everything you've done for us, your community, Israel."

"What are you saying? I'm fired, you have no need for me anymore, and you're pouring on the compliments to get me ready for the ax? "Don't be ridiculous, Meshek. I'll be direct. I heard you've arranged for the Quessem family to visit with Dan Atai and his family. Don't say anything just yet. You know this is out of protocol, especially with a family from the West Bank, Tulkarm. We've just gone in there and have been building the barrier. They've never been happy about our existence, but now? Forget it.

"What's this all about? Are you getting soft in your old age, Meshek? Not a good idea to be soft with these people. You know that better than anyone. Remember some of our handlers—Avi, Etan? I'm sure you do. They weakened for just a moment, and it cost them their lives. It takes just one break in the link, and it's over for you and who knows who else. You may even be putting the Atais in danger.

"So, what's the deal? Why these people? I should put the kibosh on this right now, but I want to hear what you have to say." Glaser sat there without a smile or a sneer—nothing but a cold, blank stare that said, "convince me."

Meshek had been standing the whole time, but now he needed to sit. He moved a chair closer to Glaser and sat. He said nothing and looked like he was thinking about how he would choose his words. "Look, do you know the story between these two men?" Meshek asked.

"No, why don't you tell me. I would love to hear this tale. I'm sure it will eat away at my heart."

صداقة يدىدوت صداقة يدىدوت صداقة يدىدوت صداقة يدىدوت

صداقة ידידות صداقة ידידות صداقة ידידות صداقة ידידות

"Go ahead, be sarcastic, but at least hear me out. Give me the opportunity to explain the situation before you make any comments, okay?" Meshek was losing patience, but he knew he had to maintain his composure or this entire plan would disintegrate.

"Continue, Meshek. I'm listening." Glaser had a smirk as he stared at Meshek. He seemed to be enjoying this cat-and-mouse game.

Meshek ignored his smirk and began the story. He didn't want to take up too much of the supervisor's valuable time, so he was going to keep it brief.

"Mr. Atai and Mr. Quessem were childhood friends. The Quessem family lived in Tulkarm. Quessem's Abi got to know Atai's Aba through his carpet shop when he traveled into Netanya to sell his produce. The families became very close, but that was to be short-lived. As you may remember, there were many incidents, which caused families like the Quessems to be turned away at the checkpoint. They stayed in Tulkarm, and that was the breakup of the friendship. End of story.

"It was merely by chance that Atai's son met Quessem's son who was looking for the carpet shop owner who had known his Abi years ago. He thought that man may provide some information about the whereabouts of his family. When I saw Quessem and Atai face one another and the look they gave one another, it was apparent that they weren't strangers. There was something warm and familiar when their eyes met. When the time was right, I confronted Quessem about their meeting, and he told me the whole story.

"So there it is. Are you satisfied or do you want more detail? I just

صداقة ידידות صداقة ידידות صداقة ידידות صداقة ידידות

صداقة يدِيدות صداقة يدِيدوت صداقة يدِيدوت صداقة يدِيدوت

thought it would be all right to give them some time to reminisce about their past. It was nothing more. I'm posting soldiers outside the house, and when it's time, they will leave and have an escort back to Tulkarm. These people are not terrorists; they are just angry at having their house demolished. Look, I know they don't love us but they're decent, not your typical West Bank citizen."

"Well, that is a fine story, Meshek, and you did a great job of telling it. They're just angry at having their house demolished," Glaser said sarcastically. Meshek stared back, not amused. "Are you kidding me? They're not terrorists, you say. Can you guarantee that? Can you guarantee that to the people of Netanya?" Glaser demanded. He was losing his patience and stood up to leave.

Meshek couldn't stay silent. "Let's be realistic. They've been held by us for several days. If they had a plan or knew of someone who had a plan, don't you think it would have happened by now or that we would have found out? How was Quessem to know that Atai was his long-lost friend? You and I both know that would be impossible. So what's your theory now?"

"You bring up a good point. I'm curious though as to when your compassion took precedence over the safety of your people."

"I can't explain to you why, but I do know that this is unlike other situations. I just feel differently about this. There is something about these two men who seemed so genuine in their feelings for one another. If you were there, you would understand."

"And we all lived happily ever after. Yeah, yeah, yeah. Go ahead with your plan, but you'd better be damn sure everything is in place and that nothing—and I mean *nothing*—will go wrong. Do you understand me?"

صداقة يدِيدوت صداقة يدِيدوت صداقة يدِيدوت صداقة يدِيدوت

صداقة يديدوت صداقة يديدوت صداقة يديدوت صداقة يديدوت

"Of course I do, and I can assure you I have everything worked out. Please trust me."

"It's not *you* I don't trust. I still don't like it, and I don't agree with it. You're taking a big risk. I hope you don't regret it. You are to stay in touch with me at all times until the soldiers have escorted them from the house and they are on their way back to Tulkarm. You hear me?"

"It will be done exactly as you request," Meshek promised.

"I'll talk to you later. I need a cup of coffee." Glaser got up, walked to the door, and slammed it behind him.

Nothing better go wrong, Meshek thought. He sat down, going over everything once again. In one hour, the Quessems would be on their way to the Atai house.

صداقة يديدوت صداقة يديدوت صداقة يديدوت صداقة يديدوت

Chapter 13

Joshua and Ahmed were in the courtyard playing soccer. They were both very competitive players having been active in their community teams. While Joshua was moving the ball away from Ahmed, he suddenly stopped.

"Come on, Joshua, don't stop now." Ahmed kept moving his legs around trying to entice the other boy to continue. Joshua began kicking the ball around and out of the way of Ahmed.

"Hey, what will you do when you get back to Tulkarm?" Ahmed tried to look at Joshua and the ball at the same time.

"What do you think I'm going to do? I'll see my jiddo and sister and help my parents get settled into our new home, our temporary new home."

"No, I mean what's the one thing you're looking forward to doing that you haven't done since you've been in Netanya?" Ahmed stopped moving, looked around, and saw a bench. He walked over to it and sat down.

Joshua set the ball aside and did the same. "Why did you stop?"

"You asked me a question, and I wanted to answer it without shouting across the courtyard to you."

"Okay, so what did you miss while you were here?"

"Joshua, you might find this strange, but everything I've done

صداقة يدِيدوت صداقة يدِيدوت صداقة يدِيدوت صداقة يدِيدوت

with you has given me what I would have wanted back in Tulkarm. Does that make sense?"

"It kind of does, but, okay, here's my interpretation of what you just said. You don't have anything to look forward to because you have done it with me here in Netanya. Is that right?"

"Yes, you do understand somewhat. I miss my jiddo and sister and my friends, but you have given me a generous friendship these past few days. And it was at a time when I really needed someone. That's what makes us spiritual brothers."

"Don't get sappy, Ahmed, or I'm going to cry, boo hoo."

"I'm sure you will, Joshua. You're such a sentimental crybaby."

They both laughed and as he said that, Joshua put his arm around Ahmed and repeated, "My spiritual brother. I like that because even though we will be separated by miles, we can be brothers and friends in the spiritual sense, right?"

"Exactly; we'll have an unbreakable bond." They both smiled at one another.

Ahmed picked up the ball put it in front of his foot and kicked. Joshua took the cue and joined in. The game was on once again. The playing went on under the hot sun.

Joshua stopped. "Do you want something to drink? I'm going in to get some juice. Do you want a glass?"

"That would be great. I could use something for my thirst." Ahmed sat on the courtyard bench waiting for Joshua to return. He put his hands in his pockets and pulled out a worn and crumpled piece of paper. Opening it he realized it was a flyer from one of the Hamas when he was in the marketplace in Tulkarm. He was

صداقة يدِيدوت صداقة يدِيدوت صداقة يدِيدوت صداقة يدِيدوت

صداقة يديدوت صداقة يديدوت صداقة يديدوت صداقة يديدوت

in such a hurry that he had jammed it into his pocket and forgot about it—or did he?

I did change clothes the other day. I must have pulled it out and stuffed it into my pocket without ever looking at it. Who would believe me? Certainly not Joshua and his family. After all, he was wearing a pair of Joshua's shorts that he loaned him so his clothes could be washed. Ahmed had remembered he had the paper, than he took it out of his shorts and put it back into the pocket of the shorts loaned to him. He hadn't read it, but he questioned himself on why he hadn't just tossed it away.

Ahmed felt guilty knowing he had this piece of paper while enjoying the hospitality of the Atais. He promised himself he would get rid of it when he got back to Tulkarm. He didn't want to leave this behind in Netanya. He shoved it back into his pocket as he saw Joshua approaching.

"Here you are, Ahmed."

"Thanks. It's really hot out here, and I didn't realize how thirsty and sweaty I was."

"That's what happens when you play soccer. Time goes by quickly, and you forget about being thirsty or sweaty." Ahmed gulped the juice down. "Juice tastes extra special when you really need it. That was so good."

"Do you want more? I'll go get it. That might not be enough to keep you from getting dehydrated."

"No, I'm good. Honest. That was just right."

Joshua drank his juice quickly. "Ah, delicious. Let's go inside and wait for your parents to arrive. It's almost time for their arrival."

"Is it really? Oh my gosh, I feel so nervous." Ahmed felt unsure

صداقة يديدوت صداقة يديدوت صداقة يديدوت صداقة يديدوت

صداقة يدّدوت صداقة يدّدوت صداقة يدّدوت صداقة يدّدوت

of himself and anxious, but he shouldn't have. These were his parents he was going to see, and they would shortly go back to the lives they had together.

"Ahmed, you needn't be nervous. You should be happy and rejoicing at being with your parents again. This is what you were determined to do, and it happened."

"You're right, Joshua. It is a happy occasion. I'll pull myself together."

"Good, now let's get cleaned up so we can be presentable for your parents." Joshua and Ahmed went running into the house. Ahmed put his arm out to slow Joshua down. "What is it, is something wrong?"

"No, do you smell that wonderful aroma? Is that the most delicious scent? It reminds me of my home and my Ommy's kitchen."

"My Ima must be preparing the meal for your parents' visit. You know she's a good cook."

"True, but the fragrance is so familiar to me, and it makes me both happy and sad at the same time."

Before Joshua had a chance to respond to Ahmed, Ima walked into the room. "Boys, please get into the bathroom and get cleaned up. Do you see what you look like? Better yet, take turns showering. Ahmed, I'll give you your freshly cleaned clothes. This way you will be able to wear them back to Tulkarm this evening. I'll put them on Joshua's bed. Now hurry up. Your parents will be here shortly. I don't want them seeing you this way and thinking I've neglected you."

صداقة يدّدوت صداقة يدّدوت صداقة يدّدوت صداقة يدّدوت

صداقة يديدوت صداقة يديدوت صداقة يديدوت صداقة يديدوت

"Yes, of course, Mrs. Atai. Come on, Joshua. Let's get cleaned up."

"You can go first. I'll be waiting in the kitchen with Ima."

On Ahmed's way to the bathroom, Mrs. Atai handed him his freshly laundered clothing. She put her arm around him and gave him a hug. "This is a special day, isn't it, Ahmed?" She gave him a smile that was warm and loving. If you need anything, I'll be in the kitchen."

"Thanks Mrs. Atai, for everything." Ahmed looked away as he said this. He didn't want her to see his tears and to think he was unhappy.

While Ahmed was bathing, Joshua used the time to help his Ima in the kitchen. He took the dishes from the cabinet and was about to bring them to the dining room table. "No, Joshua, today we're using our good china. Get the plates from the cabinet in the dining room please. Do the same and get the good silverware and goblets. This is a special occasion, and we must treat it as such."

Obeying his Ima's request, he counted out the fine china plates that she kept for special occasions like this one and opened the draw to retrieve the silverware. He opened the top cabinet door and took out the beautiful cut-crystal goblets. Joshua then organized each place setting for his family and guests. He stood back and took a look at the table.

"Ima, come in here and tell me what you think." Joshua stared at the table, proud of the job he had completed.

"Well, I'm impressed, Joshua Atai. I think I'll have you be my assistant for every event held in our home."

"Really? Sounds good." He followed her back to the kitchen

صداقة يديدوت صداقة يديدوت صداقة يديدوت صداقة يديدوت

صداقة يديدوت صداقة يديدوت صداقة يديدوت صداقة يديدوت

and sat at the table. "Is there anything else I can do for you?" he asked.

"Not at the moment, everything's good."

"Ima, can I ask you something—and please be honest with me?"

"Of course, Joshua, what is it?"

"I've known Ahmed for such a short time, but I feel we have gotten to be close friends quickly."

"Excuse me for interrupting. That may be true, but remember that your friendship has been an unusual one. What you and Ahmed have been through these past several days is not a typical friendship. It has been an intense time, and that is what has made the friendship seem so close. Does that make sense to you?"

"I guess. What I'm trying to say is that while I feel we have shared so much in such a short time, I really don't know him."

"Does that bother you? It seems like it does. Joshua, it would be impossible for you to really know him or anyone else in such a short amount of time. This is not as strange as it seems to you. What are you really trying to say?"

"It bothers me a little bit because I wonder if I would feel the same way if he was Israeli."

"Oh, so there may be a bit of mistrust or suspicion that you're feeling about Ahmed?" *Ima sure is a smart woman,* Joshua was thinking. She knows exactly how I feel without me even saying it, but I will.

"Yes, I suppose it has to do with his being a Palestinian, and I know I shouldn't be thinking this way. This is not the way Aba taught me, and I have guilt for feeling this way."

"Joshua, just keep what your Aba taught you close to your heart.

صداقة يديدوت صداقة يديدوت صداقة يديدوت صداقة يديدوت

صداقة ידדות صداقة ידידות صداقة ידידות صداقة ידידות

Don't stray from his teachings. He taught you the right way. He is a man of compassion and great understanding and he wants you to be the same. Enjoy the last hours of Ahmed's visit before—"

Before she could finish her thought, Ahmed stood in the doorway of the kitchen. "Go ahead, Joshua, I'm finished.

"What a handsome and clean boy you are, Ahmed. Now you look ready for your parents' arrival," Mrs. Atai told him. "Joshua, if the Quessems arrive on time, you only have about forty-five minutes to get cleaned and ready."

"Ima, I'm going."

"Ahmed, please sit down until Joshua is finished. Would you like something to drink?"

"I don't think so, Mrs. Atai. I think I'm a little nervous right now. I'll just sit here and wait for Joshua."

Mr. Atai came in from the garden. "Hello, Ahmed. Are you excited about seeing your parents? I know they will be so happy to be with you again."

"Yes, Mr. Atai, I'm excited and nervous. This will be the best day ever."

"Good. You know I'm excited—and nervous too—seeing my old friend. I think once we say our hellos and embrace, we will have a wonderful visit." Ahmed nodded and smiled at Mr. Atai. "My darling, Adiva, whatever you're making smells absolutely delicious. This is going to be quite a feast."

"Dan, you love everything I make. You're very easy to please, and that's what makes cooking so enjoyable."

"I'm done." Joshua came running into the kitchen. "How do I look? Do I pass inspection?"

صداقة ידידות صداقة ידידות صداقة ידידות صداقة ידידות

صداقة يديدوت صداقة يديدوت صداقة يديدوت صداقة يديدوت

"Magnificent, a real sabra, Joshua." Dan Atai looked proudly at his only son. "Okay gentlemen, why don't we sit down in the living room and wait for our guests to arrive. It's almost that time, and if I know Meshek, he will have them here on the second."

Joshua said, "Ahmed, want to play a game of chess while we wait?"

"Sure, that will keep my mind busy so I don't watch the clock."

Joshua went to his room and came back with the game. He and Ahmed set it up on the teak table that was near the corner window. He knew this would give them a good view of the street so they could see Ahmed's parents pull up to the house. They sat at the table and began their game while Mr. Atai picked up a book to read from the vast collection of books that were held in the floor-to-ceiling bookcases.

Dan Atai was a reader of everything. There wasn't a subject he wasn't interested in, and he could speak with authority about many of them. Every so often, he raised his eyes above his glasses to check for the visitors. The book was not holding his interest as he thought it would. He too was anxious about the arrival of his good friend from the past.

As Joshua attempted to make his next move, he looked at the window and saw a serious-looking black car pull up to the house. He grabbed Ahmed by the arm. "Look, Ahmed, they're here. Hurry let's put these pieces away so we'll be ready when Aba opens the door." Ahmed grabbed as many pieces as he could and threw them into the case with the board.

"Aba, Aba, do you see the car outside? It must be them."

"Stay calm and keep your composure. Why don't you young

صداقة يدودت صداقة يديدة صداقة يدودت صداقة يدودت صداقة يدودت

men stand with me when they approach the door, and we will greet them together?"

"Okay, Aba." "Yes, Mr. Atai." They both responded at the same time.

Chapter 14

Just at that moment there was a heavy banging at the door. All of them walked toward it without rushing to swing it open. Mr. Atai turned the lock, opening the door to the face of Mr. Meshek Geller. Alongside him were two soldiers serving as escorts for the Quessems.

"Shalom, Dan."

"Shalom," Dan responded.

Mr. Geller then proceeded to introduce the two soldiers to him. He explained that they would be standing outside his front door until it was time to escort the Quessem family on the drive to Tulkarm. Dan thanked him and raised his arm to invite Mr. and Mrs. Quessem into the house. Before Dan closed the door, he thought it would be only proper to ask Meshek and the soldiers if they would like a beverage. The soldiers said they were carrying canteens.

"Very nice of you to ask, Dan, but I must get back to the office. I will return at seven o'clock. I hope that will be enough time for you and your family to get reacquainted with the Quessem family."

"As I have said before, this is very generous of you, and I'm sure we will have time to reminisce. See you at seven o'clock." He turned around to close the door and saw that his wife had made the Quessem family comfortable. They were sitting on the couch

صداقة ﻳﺪﻳﺪﻭﺕ صداقة ﻳﺪﻳﺪﻭﺕ صداقة ﻳﺪﻳﺪﻭﺕ صداقة ﻳﺪﻳﺪﻭﺕ

while Mrs. Atai told them how happy she and Dan were that they could visit with them.

"Please, forgive my lack of manners, Ghali, and—"

"This is my wife, Barirah," Ghali said to help Dan out.

"Let me start again. Ghali and Barirah, this is my wife, Adiva. And Adiva, this is my childhood friend Ghali and his wife, Barirah. I believe you met my son Joshua at the station."

"Of course. This has been quite a surprise by your city and security people allowing us to visit with you like this."

"I was surprised too, but a miracle has happened so I don't question it. I'm just so happy you are here." Dan motioned to Ahmed and Joshua to join them. Mr. Quessem called Ahmed over, and he and Mrs. Quessem pulled him close to them and hugged and kissed him.

"I want to say this in front of all of you," Mr. Quessem announced. "First, I want to thank my good friend Daniel and his family for taking care of my precious son. Second, Ahmed, you are a brave boy for undertaking this journey by yourself. This could have ended tragically had it not been for Allah watching over you and sending you Joshua. Dan, once more our lives have crossed each other's paths, and fate has brought our sons together."

"Life can be so very strange; sometimes we shouldn't try to overanalyze it. Let's go into the dining room and sit down to a delicious meal my lovely wife has prepared in honor of your visit."

The Quessems followed the Atais into the spacious dining room. The table was beautifully set, and each one took a seat. On a buffet in the corner sat many pictures of the family, but several

صداقة ﻳﺪﻳﺪﻭﺕ صداقة ﻳﺪﻳﺪﻭﺕ صداقة ﻳﺪﻳﺪﻭﺕ صداقة ﻳﺪﻳﺪﻭﺕ

صداقة يديدوت صداقة يديدوت صداقة يديدوت صداقة يديدوت

pictures stood out. They were of the same person, Avram Atai, the son they had lost.

One picture in particular caught the eye of Mr. Quessem. "Who is the handsome boy in the uniform, Dan?" Dan's face took on a pained look, and he didn't answer right away. "Did I say something wrong? I am sorry if I did. I don't want to spoil this wonderful occasion."

Mrs. Quessem put her hand on her husband's arm as if to say that he did nothing wrong. Mrs. Atai walked into the dining room with a platter to begin the meal but noticed the silence in the room.

Dan finally spoke. "Adiva, they wanted to know who the boy in the picture is. You didn't ask the wrong question. You wouldn't have known the situation. The boy was our older son, Avram. He was on duty during our Passover holiday when he was killed."

"May you and your family be blessed. This should never happen to anyone. To lose a child is life's greatest loss. He was a very handsome boy."

"I appreciate your friendship." Dan rose and walked closer to Ghali Quessem. They embraced and held on to one another for a long time. Dan patted him on the back and sat down. "Now let's say our prayers and then begin this great feast, shall we?"

There were several minutes of silence, and then both men looked up to signal the start of the meal for their family members. Both women excused themselves to begin the first course. Joshua and Ahmed stared at one another and smiled. The platters were set down on the table, and Barirah went into the kitchen to get the bread.

"We are lucky men, aren't we?" Dan said to Ghali.

صداقة يديدوت صداقة يديدوت صداقة يديدوت صداقة يديدوت

صداقة يديدوت صداقة يديدوت صداقة يديدوت صداقة يديدوت

"We are truly blessed both with wives and family," Ghali said in agreement. The women sat down and each passed a platter to her husband first, spooning out generous helpings for them.

"So tell me, what do you do in Tulkarm? I haven't kept up with news from there, but I do know there has been some building in the West Bank. From my memory of it, it was a city filled with merchants and families. Has it changed much? I mean other than the political climate? Are there any of the old shopkeepers there?" Dan seemed interested in knowing about his friend's city.

"Times have changed. The shops are there, but now there is a large marketplace where I bring my fruits, vegetables, and olives for sale. The merchants sell a large variety of fruits and vegetables, meats, drinks, and nuts. In another section, we have the clothing and fabric merchants and so on. Our home was within walking distance from the market. Now, well, it's a different story. But we will not dwell on that.

"It's been a very long time, Dan, and I never thought we would be in each other's lives again. To think that our sons have been responsible for this is something I couldn't imagine."

"You have a brave son to have taken on a journey to come to Netanya thinking he would be able to find you, and then to meet Joshua … it is too much to comprehend. We can thank our boys for bringing us together if only for a short time."

While Dan and Ghali were talking, their wives continued their meal and listened to their husbands' conversation. Adiva didn't want to pry too much into Barirah's life, but she was uncomfortable sitting there in silence. She was a woman who was used to socializing with the sophisticated and worldly artistic community. Yet she

صداقة يديدوت صداقة يديدوت صداقة يديدوت صداقة يديدوت

صداقة يدِدوت صداقة يدِدوت صداقة يدِدوت صداقة يدِدوت

could still appreciate the type of woman Barirah was—that of a dutiful and obedient wife.

Maybe if I start making conversation, she will become more talkative, Adiva thought.

Meanwhile, Joshua and Ahmed didn't let the conversation stop them from devouring the first part of the meal.

Dan realized that neither he nor his friend had taken a bite, and he wanted to show his wife their appreciation for the meal. "Let's enjoy this delicious meal, shall we, Ghali?"

"Of course. This looks wonderful, and I recognize the kafta and maqluba lamb that you made." Mr. Quessem lifted a forkful of the lamb and potatoes to his mouth. "You are one of us, Adiva. You have captured the flavors of this dish. Thank you for spending so much time preparing this for us."

"It was a pleasure to prepare this meal, and I have Ahmed to thank. He wrote out the ingredients as he remembered them from his Ommy."

"Ahmed, I had no idea you paid attention to such things. I thought your job was to eat and enjoy your Ommy's cooking." Everyone laughed except Ahmed, who seemed embarrassed by his Abi's comment. He faced down toward his lap and waited for the laughter to stop.

Joshua gently kicked his foot under the table, and Ahmed looked up. "I wish I knew as much as you do about food, Ahmed. If I ever have to feed myself, I'll be in trouble. Either that or I'll have to look you up." Ahmed smiled, and he knew Joshua was trying to help him shake off the self-consciousness he felt at being singled out.

صداقة يدِدوت صداقة يدِدوت صداقة يدِدوت صداقة يدِدوت

صداقة يديدות صداقة يديدות صداقة يديدوت صداقة يديدوت

"I'm sure if and when the time comes, Joshua, you will be quite self-sufficient."

"Let's finish this luscious course so we can enjoy the rest of this special meal," Dan said as he tried to direct everyone back to the task of eating. Except for the oohs and aahs as each course was brought in, the rest of the meal was eaten with little conversation. Dan directed Ghali into the living room while their wives waited in the kitchen for the dishes Joshua and Ahmed were helping to clear.

صداقة يديدوت صداقة يديدوت صداقة يديدوت صداقة يديدوت

Chapter 15

"Please have a seat. I have something to show you, something you may have long forgotten."

"I'm looking forward to it, Dan. You know I have to tell you, I still see the remains of the young boy I met many years ago."

"Really? I feel like I have the face of a very old and worn-out man. I think the memory of our friendship is doing funny things to your mind, eh?"

"No, it's true. You still have touches of the youthful boy I knew."

"Very good, then I accept your compliment. I'll be right back."

Mr. Quessem looked around the room at the paintings, family pictures, the coziness of the furniture, and the comfortable chair he was sitting in. He felt a sense of sadness overwhelm him when he thought about going back to Tulkarm. It wouldn't be the same without his family home. Of course, they would make do with the apartment his wife had rented for them. He was grateful that she had the calm presence and courage to make arrangements ahead of time. The loss of their home had happened, but they were prepared.

"Here it is. Are you ready? Let's see if you remember this picture." Dan was smiling proudly that he had been able to hold on to the picture and that he had placed it in a corner of his dresser draw for safekeeping. Dan handed the picture to Mr. Quessem.

"Praise Allah. I do remember this picture. Look at how

innocent and happy we were. Our arms around one another and smiling. We almost look like brothers. In fact, do you remember we were walking down the street when we bought a drink, and someone stopped and asked us if we were brothers?"

"I do remember that very clearly. Do you think we still look like brothers?"

"Perhaps, but it's hard to tell under my beard isn't it? We were so unaware of the world surrounding us and how it would interfere in our friendship. We didn't have a care, did we, Dan?"

"None. Our biggest worry was what time we would meet each other and what games we would play. Those were good times and as worry free as it could be in those days."

"Is this the only picture you have of us? Could you make a copy and send it to me? I will write my address before it is time to go. If we're lucky, it will get through before someone intercepts it to see if it is something legitimate."

"Of course I'll make a copy for you. It may be the only way we'll be able to preserve the happy memories of our friendship."

Joshua and Ahmed walked into the living room. Joshua said, "Ima and Mrs. Quessem have finished with the dishes. They'll be here in a few minutes."

"Very good Joshua."

"When the ladies come in why don't we all go and sit in the courtyard garden? We can have our beverage and dessert out there."

"That sounds splendid. It would be nice to get some fresh air. We have been isolated for several days, but it seems like months," Mr. Quessem offered.

"I know. History has not been good to us, has it? But let's not dwell on that; we're here to enjoy our visit together. That's what is important."

"Dan, you give me the little hope that I have. Going back to Tulkarm without our family home is devastating for us. That home was our life. My Abi built it, and I was so proud to help him. Now there is nothing left but rubble. Abi and my daughter, Ayat, took what possessions we could salvage with them. At least that is what Barirah has told me."

"Ghali, you and Barirah will build again. You are both strong. The troublemakers always harm the innocent, the people who work for a living, pray, and try to raise their families—and that goes for both sides."

"I will keep your words close to my heart, and I will build again. I am determined to give my family the home that they deserve. Our family home meant everything to us. Thank you for your kind words and your encouragement."

"Anytime my friend, anytime." Dan moved closer and patted Ghali on the back just as their wives entered the room.

"How nice that you're having such a happy visit," Mrs. Atai commented. Dan got up and cleared his throat, visibly uncomfortable that his wife may have seen him showing affection to his friend.

"Ladies, gentleman, boys, let's go into the courtyard and relax. We'll have some coffee and a sweet and continue with this lovely visit." They followed Mrs. Atai out to the courtyard. Dan moved some benches and chairs to form a circle, making it easier for conversation.

Mrs. Atai excused herself and motioned to Mrs. Quessem to go into the kitchen to prepare the coffee and cake. It was an unusually

صداقة يديدوت صداقة يديدوت صداقة يديدوت صداقة يديدوت

warm day. The overhead sun seemed to target the courtyard, but a cool breeze found its way across the seated friends at just the right time.

Dan stood up. "Excuse me for a moment. I wanted to see if our security guests would like a beverage." He walked through the black, wrought-iron gate of the courtyard and circled to the front of the house. As he walked toward the door, the soldiers were taken by surprise. They were leaning on two railings that were on each side of the door, looking more relaxed than soldiers who were on duty.

"Sabras, it's rather warm out here, and I thought you might like a beverage; I'm sure your canteens have emptied out."

They seemed surprised at Dan's generous offering. "Thank you, sir, but we have our supply of water with us. That will be sufficient."

"Very well then, we'll see you later." Within a few minutes, Dan was back in the courtyard sitting with Ghali. "Sorry for the interruption. Now tell me about your work, your life, everything! I want to know all the things I have missed with you."

"Dan, I had some land where I farmed citrus fruits, lemons, oranges, and I grew wonderful sweet, plump dates. My Abi's olive trees were old and beautiful. If this was a visit that I had planned, I would have brought you a basketful. It took a while, but my Abi cultivated the land. When I was old enough, I helped him continue to build on the crops he had started.

"We had some beautiful crops. We sold them in the marketplace in Tulkarm, but it was too difficult to try and sell them in Netanya. Sometimes the checkpoints would be open to us, and more times than not, people from Tulkarm were turned away.

"As I had already mentioned to you, my Abi built our home

صداقة يديدوت صداقة يديدوت صداقة يديدوت صداقة يديدوت

صداقة يدیدوت صداقة يدیدوت صداقة يدیدوت صداقة يدیدوت

and I helped whenever repairs were needed. When the repairs were made, I was so proud to have had a part in helping him. Abi made me feel like a genius. It was a home that had a small courtyard, but you could see our crops surrounding it. It was a fairly peaceful existence except when we could hear explosions and gunfire in the distance. Abi and I enjoyed coming back to our home from a busy and noisy day at the marketplace.

"My devoted wife had the most delicious meals waiting for us each evening. Ahmed had his friends and was involved in soccer. It was a good life, and it will be again, praise Allah."

"You have been blessed, and you will have that life again. How is your Abi? How old is he now—in his seventies like my Aba?"

"He's seventy-two and in good health, although I think this episode with our home will affect him greatly. When they began the demolition, he stayed calm and tried to keep me from shouting, but he couldn't do it. I was so angry and frustrated that I couldn't control or stop what was happening. I didn't feel like myself.

"At that moment, I had become a different person and was feeling hatred that I had not felt before. Abi is a gentle man and taught me much like your Aba taught you about kindness and compassion. I fear that I have shortened his life now that Barirah and I have been taken away."

"I'm glad to hear his health is good." Dan avoided Ghali's comment about the demolition shortening his Abi's life. "How well I remember him coming to my Aba's shop. You described him well. He was a gentle, soft-spoken man. When you do see him, please tell him Daniel was asking about him."

صداقة يدیدوت صداقة يدیدوت صداقة يدیدوت صداقة يدیدوت

صداقة ﻳﺪﻳﺪﻭﺕ صداقة ﻳﺪﻳﺪﻭﺕ صداقة ﻳﺪﻳﺪﻭﺕ صداقة ﻳﺪﻳﺪﻭﺕ

"Of course I will. Now what about you, Dan? Are you the carpet man too, like your Aba?"

"I took over the business for almost thirty years, but with the big department stores and carpet and floor stores, the old-time carpet merchant is becoming obsolete. I'm closing the business. I rarely go in, and when I do, it's just to check on the inventory I have left.

"I've sold a good amount of it, and in a few weeks that will be it. I'm not sure what I'll do next. I'm too young to retire. I need something to do, but I'll figure it out. Adiva has her art gallery, and it's doing very well. It keeps her very busy, and she loves it. It's good medicine for her and helps her to keep her mind on her art and not on Avram." As the words came out, Dan regretted mentioning Avram. He wanted to keep the conversation about Adiva, but it just slipped out.

"It is a difficult situation, and work helps each of us get through the day. I'm happy to hear you're both doing well."

Mrs. Atai came out with a tray of coffee and cups. Mrs. Quessem was right behind her with a platter of assorted desserts, some Palestinian and some Israeli. Mr. Atai moved the table closer so they could all share in this after-meal treat.

"Your hospitality is overwhelming, and you have done so much for us in such a short time. This looks delicious. Thank you for including some of our favorite dishes," Ghali said. Barirah nodded and smiled in agreement with her husband.

"I'm going to get something special that I think you and Dan will enjoy," Adiva said as she excused herself for a brief moment, then quickly returned to the courtyard with a worn photo album.

صداقة ﻳﺪﻳﺪﻭﺕ صداقة ﻳﺪﻳﺪﻭﺕ صداقة ﻳﺪﻳﺪﻭﺕ صداقة ﻳﺪﻳﺪﻭﺕ

صداقة يدّيدوت صداقة يدّيدوت صداقة يدّيدوت صداقة يدّيدوت

"Here, Dan, you and Ghali might want to look at these together. Barirah and I will have our dessert in the kitchen."

Ghali wasn't sure what photos he was going to see that would make him feel any better. He knew he shouldn't look at them but he couldn't help himself. He wanted to relive those memories of childhood. Ghali couldn't get his mind off of what awaited him in Tulkarm, and he was trying his best to keep his anger from being directed at Dan and his family.

Ahmed and Joshua excused themselves after eating their dessert to continue a game of soccer. They were involved in their game and unaware of what was going on in the courtyard near the kitchen.

"Ghali, move your chair closer, and we'll take a look into the past." Instead of getting up, Ghali moved to the chair closest to Dan. He took a sip of his coffee and waited for Dan to turn the cover.

"Well, look at this, Ghali. These are pictures of my Aba's shop when he first opened it."

"Everything was so new and your Aba looked so proud, smiling and pointing up at the shop's name. Is this you in this picture?" Ghali pointed to another picture at the top of the page.

"I'm afraid it is, so young and innocent. I'm standing there like *I* own the shop and not Aba." Dan laughed. Ghali didn't join him in the laughter.

"Life was different, wasn't it, Dan? At least it was different for my family."

"Why are you saying that? You and your Abi made frequent trips to Netanya. You didn't meet with the kind of resistance that exists today."

صداقة يدّيدوت صداقة يدّيدوت صداقة يدّيدوت صداقة يدّيدوت

صداقة يدِيدوت صداقة يدِيدوت صداقة يدِيدوت صداقة يدِيدوت

"I guess it's difficult for you to understand, Dan. You're secure, aren't you? You're safe and don't have to stay up nights worrying if your home will be taken away from you—not only taken away, but demolished for good. Every stone and all the concrete that my Abi and I poured is reduced to dust. You haven't had to deal with that kind of disrespect."

"Wait," Dan interrupted. "What are you saying? We're safe, really? Relatively speaking maybe, but I never know if something will happen when I sit in a restaurant or travel by bus. Our lives are precarious Ghali like every human being."

"Please, I want to finish what I have to say. When I go to Tulkarm tonight, my family goes home to Barirah's sister's apartment, and while I'm grateful we will have a place to go for the night, my family will be stuffed in there like a herd of cows. Tomorrow we go to the apartment my wife was smart enough to get for us.

"Where will I grow my crops? How will I earn a living for my family? Barirah might have to take in sewing if she is fortunate to have any garments to sew. I'm not a young man, do you hear me? I don't have the energy to start from the beginning. We are treated like worthless soil." Ghali's voice was loud enough that Ahmed and Joshua came running around the corner of the courtyard.

Barirah and Adiva looked from the window, not wanting to interfere. Ahmed could see his Abi's veins stretching the length of his neck. He hadn't seen his father this upset. When Ghali turned and saw his son standing there with Joshua, he turned back around and looked at Dan.

Dan looked deeply into Ghali's eyes, hoping this would calm

صداقة يدِيدوت صداقة يدِيدوت صداقة يدِيدوت صداقة يدِيدوت

صداقة يديدوت صداقة يديدوت صداقة يديدوت صداقة يديدوت

him even for a moment, then he spoke quietly. "Ghali, is it my fault what has happened? We have spoken about this many times, especially when we were young. Do I think it's morally wrong that people's homes are being demolished? Of course I do, but I also have to look at the root of what caused the wall to be built.

"Remember, my son was one of the victims of an explosion, and the Israeli response to these kinds of incidents was to build a wall to minimize the people infiltrating Israel with explosives."

"Dan, I am frustrated, and I know we both walk a tightrope between good and evil. I just don't understand why homes have to be demolished. The wall could still be built. We would just be closer to it, that's all. You are my friend. This I believe. You are a sincere and compassionate person, but you and I know that this is not true of our people."

"Ahmed, Joshua, come here," Dan said sternly. The boys walked hesitantly toward their fathers. "Have a seat. You are old enough to hear this. Two old friends are having a discussion about the unfairness of what happens in life. Sometimes when we voice our feelings and thoughts, we become emotionally charged and our voices get louder. We are still good friends, nothing has changed, all right?"

"You understand, Ahmed?" Ghali asked his son.

"Yes, Abi."

"Joshua?"

"Yes, Aba."

"Good. Now go back to your game." Ghali and Dan were convinced their sons understood what they were told, but didn't believe the friendship hadn't suffered.

صداقة يديدوت صداقة يديدوت صداقة يديدوت صداقة يديدوت

صداقة يديدوت صداقة يديدوت صداقة يديدوت صداقة يديدوت

"Ghali, have you spoken with a lawyer about compensation for your land and house?"

"Lawyer? How would I do that? No one approached me about that. We were given several weeks to get our belongings and go. There wasn't any mention about lawyers, compensation, anything."

"I read in the newspaper when this wall was proposed that the people affected would be compensated. I know it's not the same as having your home, but this could help you to get some land and build another one."

"Why wasn't I told? They can't be trusted. They just want to see what they can get away with. They must think I am a stupid, ignorant man."

"Calm down, Ghali. Even the Israelis make mistakes." A faint smile came across Ghali's face, which managed to stifle his anger. He understood Dan's sarcasm. "When Meshek comes to pick you up, I will speak to him about your situation. This is not right, and you deserve compensation to rebuild. I will see to it."

"Dan, I appreciate you getting involved, but I don't want you to put yourself under any suspicion because you are going out of your way for a Palestinian. You know how suspicious they get, just like my people. No one trusts anyone. We are all collaborators!"

Ghali and Dan laughed and put their arms around one another, patting each other on the back. Adiva had a glimpse of what was happening outside and pulled Barirah close to her as she pointed toward the glass doors.

Barirah clapped her hands together like a little girl filled with excitement about a special secret. "Let's go join our husbands."

Adiva took Barirah's hand and lead her out to the courtyard.

صداقة يديدوت صداقة يديدوت صداقة يديدوت صداقة يديدوت

صداقة يدىدوت صداقة يدىدوت صداقة يدىدوت صداقة يدىدوت

Pretending to be unaware of the discord that had taken place, Adiva asked Ghali and Dan how they were enjoying the photos. Dan also played the game of ignorance.

"This was a wonderful idea, Adiva. Ghali and I loved looking at Aba in his brand-new carpet shop."

"That was a long time ago," Adiva added. The sun was starting to dim, and she suggested they go back into the living area and continue the photo conversation.

Barirah and Adiva cleaned off the plates and desserts and assured Ghali and Dan that they would join them shortly. Ghali held the door open for them and followed Dan toward the living area. They sat down on the couch, and Dan turned the page to the next set of photos.

"Oh look at this, Ghali, two young men with their arms around one another smiling devilishly."

"Is that really us, Dan? I can't believe we were ever that young. We were probably close to Ahmed and Joshua's age."

"What were we—twelve, thirteen? We were pretty good-looking weren't we?"

"I was for sure, but I don't know about that other one." Ghali laughed.

"Haven't changed a bit, have you? As I remember, modesty was never one of your finer traits," Dan teased.

Adiva came in. "Excuse me, but I'm going to show Barirah some of the artwork. She is interested in knowing about it. I hope you don't mind."

"Not at all. Enjoy your tour."

صداقة يدىدوت صداقة يدىدوت صداقة يدىدوت صداقة يدىدوت

صداقة يديدوت صداقة يديدوت صداقة يديدوت صداقة يديدوت

Dan said, "Now let's get back to our childhood. Do you have any idea what we were doing before this picture was taken, Ghali?"

"Hmm … let me think. My Abi and I were probably visiting the shop for prayer rugs. I remember him bringing several back to Tulkarm for family and friends. Do you think your Aba wanted to have a photo of us and asked us to step outside?"

"I'm sure he wanted to have a photo of his son with his good Palestinian friend."

"Dan, I have to ask Allah for forgiveness for looking at these pictures, but I couldn't resist seeing us as young men."

"You will be forgiven because it will never happen again. I don't think any less of you, and I respect you more for your loyalty and faith."

Ghali smiled. "Thank you."

Dan continued telling the story about Aba. "Aba used to like to gloat to his friends about it. They got into many arguments. I remember he sat me down one day and told me about a good friend of his who questioned his friendliness toward your Abi. He would come and visit my Aba and sit in the back of the shop and talk until a customer came in.

"This man was in the shop one day when your Abi came alone. They had a fairly long conversation, and Aba offered him a cup of coffee and invited him to sit in the back and join them, but your Abi refused. Maybe he realized it wasn't the right thing to do with someone he didn't know. Aba never elaborated.

"Anyway, my Aba's friend became very annoyed that Aba would dare to invite your Abi to the back for coffee. Aba said he felt like a scolded child but had the courage to speak up to him.

صداقة يديدوت صداقة يديدوت صداقة يديدوت صداقة يديدوت

صداقة يديدوت صداقة يديدوت صداقة يديدوت صداقة يديدوت

He said he called him a narrow-minded zealot who would be one of the reasons there would never be peace among the Israeli and Palestinian people. They didn't speak for a long time, and Aba said he didn't care. That having someone who called himself a friend and felt that way was a friend he didn't need."

"That's quite a story, Dan. Your Aba was brave to speak up. Maybe the Shin Bet has been watching you for a long time."

"You never know, Ghali, you never know." Quite a bit of time passed as they continued to look at each photo, commenting on each one.

Adiva and Barirah came into the room. "Are you now well-schooled in art, Barirah?" Dan asked.

"Yes. Adiva is a good teacher. You have many beautiful pieces of art."

"Excuse me everyone, but time has gotten away from all of us. It's five o'clock, and we have two hours remaining."

"That reminds me, Ghali. I'm going to try and contact Meshek. I want him to know about the compensation issue in case he can bring papers or the name of someone to contact. I'll only be a minute."

"Thank you for trying," Ghali said. He asked Barirah to sit down beside him and began to explain the compensation that they were supposed to receive. Barirah smiled and sat up straight, asking him one question after another. "We must wait to hear what Dan finds out and if Mr. Geller can help us with the name of a lawyer or paperwork. This will be a way for us to purchase some land and rebuild."

"Yes, Ghali, I will be patient. I pray to Allah that we will enjoy

صداقة يديدوت صداقة يديدوت صداقة يديدوت صداقة يديدوت

a new home again for our family. Your Abi will be so happy. This will give him twenty more years," Barirah reassured him.

Dan walked to the kitchen and dialed Meshek's number. The phone rang numerous times until someone finally answered, "Shalom." "Shalom. Meshek Geller, please."

"Dan, this is Meshek. I recognized your voice. Everything all right, enjoying your visit with the Quessems?"

"Everything's fine except for one issue, and I thought perhaps you could give me an explanation."

"Yes, go ahead. Depending on what the issue is, I'll try and help."

"Thank you. Ghali and I were discussing the situation with his home's demolition, and I had talked to him about compensation that he and other families should be receiving from the Israeli government. He said he didn't know of any compensation, that nothing had been discussed with him. He was just given an order after the several weeks' notice to remove his belongings and leave his home before they arrived to do the demolition.

"Do you know anything about this compensation? I vaguely remember reading this in the news when the wall was about to be built."

"You're correct, and he should have been told that someone would contact him. However with what went on that day, I'm sure that was the last thing on the soldiers' minds. Something happened, and I will look into it."

"Are there any papers or is there someone you can give him the name of to contact about this?"

"No, let me take care of the contact and paperwork. Then I'll

صداقة يديدوت صداقة يديدوت صداقة يديدوت صداقة يديدوت

صداقة يديدوت صداقة يديدوت صداقة يديدوت صداقة يديدوت

send someone to his apartment to talk to him about completing any necessary forms to get his compensation. This will not happen overnight, and it will be decided by the court. We know where he and his family will be living. I have no explanation other than it must have been an oversight. Another thing that you mentioned bothers me."

"What's that, Meshek?"

"Families were to be given at least four weeks' notice to vacate their homes. I'm trying to figure out who contacted him and gave him only twenty-four hours to gather his family's belongings. You know what will happen? The news headlines will be shouting that Israelis are kicking out Palestinian families from their homes in twenty-four hours. They won't focus on the four weeks that is the protocol for vacating homes."

Dan whispered, "I don't know what to say about that, but I do know he's very upset about all of it. If he knows about the longer notice, I'm not sure what he would do."

"Don't mention anything about that to him. At this point it's no longer important. Just reassure him that I will take care of it, and I will talk to him on the trip back to Tulkarm. Actually, I will see all of you shortly."

"I appreciate it. Thanks for being a fair person in this situation."

"Not fair, Dan. I'm just doing what protocol says we must do. I'm protecting the Israelis, period. Shalom."

"Shalom," Dan responded. He walked to the living room, grabbing another cookie from the plate. He took Adiva's hand and walked them over to where Ghali and Barirah were sitting. They

صداقة يديدوت صداقة يديدوت صداقة يديدوت صداقة يديدوت

صداقة يديدوت صداقة يديدوت صداقة يديدوت صداقة يديدوت

sat down. The Quessems looked at Dan, waiting for something, anything, to make them feel better about their future home.

"Here's what's going to happen." Ghali and Barirah bowed their heads and waited to hear that there was nothing that could be done for them, that it was too late. "Meshek told me that he will speak to those in charge who will assign you a lawyer. The government representative will visit with you and jiddo to complete the paperwork for compensation. That's all Meshek and I know. There wasn't any talk about the amount of compensation. That will be worked out when you speak with them about your home. It may change depending on the size of your home and the plot of land it was on. I hope this is enough to give you some faith that things will work out."

Ghali and his wife slowly raised their heads at the same time and hugged each other. "That is more hope than we've been given in a long time. Thank you, Dan."

"Thank you," Barirah joined in.

Adiva stood up and stretched out her arms behind her back. "Now let's have one more cup of coffee before your escort arrives. I'll make a fresh pot. Barirah, come and join me."

Barirah was more than happy to be with Adiva in the kitchen. She sliced some more cake and filled the plate with cookies.

"I'm so glad that you and your family will be compensated. Ghali looks like a man who will be determined to build a new home for you and your children."

"Thank you, Adiva. It will take a while, especially to cultivate crops again and it depends on where we find the land to build. I have faith that Allah will be there for us."

صداقة يديدوت صداقة يديدوت صداقة يديدوت صداقة يديدوت

صداقة يديدوت صداقة يديدوت صداقة يديدوت صداقة يديدوت

Adiva smiled. "Let's bring this into the living room. Please take the platter, and I will bring the cups and saucers and pot." Barirah picked up the platter and Adiva followed.

"Come and let's sit at the game table." Dan and Ghali finished their conversation.

"We'd better do what we're told, Ghali; that is what I've been told I should say." Ghali chuckled softly and joined everyone at the table.

"It's good that your trip back will still be in daylight. That makes it easier on the travelers." Dan was trying to make conversation. He saw a silence take over the table and thought it may be that everyone was busy getting their coffee and dessert.

Barirah helped to keep the dialogue moving along. "I can't believe how fast this day has been. We have enjoyed our visit and are so thankful our son is safe."

"By the way, where are Joshua and Ahmed? I don't hear them outside or in the house." Adiva was concerned.

"They've been playing ball a good part of the day, Adiva. They're probably taking a break." Dan understood the amount of energy involved in soccer. What seemed like just kicking a ball around was an enormous amount of skill and strategy, along with quick decision-making.

Adiva ignored Dan's comments. She walked in a slow run toward Joshua's room and found it empty, then she looked out his window but did not see anyone. Dashing through the kitchen and out the doors, she found an empty courtyard. As she walked around different areas, she heard the voices of the soldiers and decided to

صداقة يديدوت صداقة يديدوت صداقة يديدوت صداقة يديدوت

صداقة يديدوت صداقة يديدوت صداقة يديدوت صداقة يديدوت

walk to the front of the house. As she got closer, she saw Joshua
and Ahmed sitting on the steps talking to the soldiers.

"Joshua, Ahmed, why are you disturbing the soldiers? I was
worried that you left the house. It's almost time for Ahmed and his
family to return to Tulkarm."

"Ima, I'm sorry but we didn't go anywhere, did we? We're still
home." Adiva looked at the soldiers. "Shalom. I apologize for these
young men."

"They didn't disturb us. We're keeping an eye on them so they
don't cause any trouble. Isn't that right?" the one soldier asked Joshua.

"That's right. See, Ima. You worried for nothing."

"I worried for something—you, Joshua. Now come inside and
have a last bite of dessert and something to drink."

"All right, if we have to."

"Bye, soldiers," Joshua and Ahmed said at the same time. The
soldiers smiled and raised their heads upward indicating good-bye.
Joshua and Ahmed obediently followed Adiva's footsteps up to the
front door.

One of the soldiers tipped his head as Joshua was about to step
into the room. "Don't give your Ima a hard time or I'll come after
you, understand, sabra?" Joshua smiled back, although he wasn't
sure if the soldier was playing a game with him.

"Yes sir, of course I'll be a good boy." As Joshua said that,
he tried to keep a straight face, but the soldier knew Joshua was
playing along with him.

"Who were you talking to, Joshua?" Dan asked.

"Just saying so long to the soldiers outside." No sooner had he
closed the door than there was a knock.

صداقة يديدوت صداقة يديدوت صداقة يديدوت صداقة يديدوت

صداقة يدود صداقة يدود صداقة يدود صداقة يدود

Joshua was still standing close enough, but Dan told him to sit down. "Joshua, I'll get that." Dan wasn't sure the soldiers would have knocked so soon after Joshua came in. He opened the door to find Meshek on the other side.

"Shalom, Dan. May I come in for a moment?"

"Of course, come in. You're a bit early for the ride back."

Meshek didn't respond as he walked in. "Shalom everyone. I hope all of you are enjoying your visit with one another. Mr. and Mrs. Quessem, I need to speak to you about the matter of compensation that Dan discussed with me earlier."

"Yes, thank you," Ghali responded hesitatingly.

"Please, all of you get comfortable and sit on the sofa. We will leave you alone," Adiva offered.

"Nonsense, you're all aware of the situation. There is nothing to hide here," Meshek assured everyone, but he had to state his position as delicately as possible. "Mr. and Mrs. Quessem, we—I should say, the Israeli government—are walking a fine line in asking Palestinian families to vacate their homes. However, the government is not throwing them out without legal representation for compensation for the homes they have lived in, and in your case, the one your Aba built.

"Many of the families we have dealt with have also built their homes, so this is not an exceptional situation. I understand that there was a gross error made in your case, and that no one discussed with you legal representation or compensation to your family for your home and land. I spoke to a source today who explained that they would give your name to a legal counsel from the government.

صداقة يدود صداقة يدود صداقة يدود صداقة يدود

صداقة يديدوت صداقة يديدوت صداقة يديدوت صداقة يديدوت

They would then assign a representative to visit you in Tulkarm and go over the necessary paperwork with you.

"I don't know how long it will take or what the compensation will be, but these are questions you can ask the representative. Then it is up to the court to decide. Do you have any other questions?"

"Excuse me, Mr. Geller, but will I have to go to court with my father for this case?"

"Possibly, since you and your father had the land and home together. Once again, these are questions you can ask."

Adiva asked, "Mr. Geller, excuse me, would you like a nice, fresh cup of coffee? I have some made."

"Thank you, Mrs. Atai. We still have some time before our ride, and that will help to keep me alert."

"Ima, Ahmed and I will be in my room."

"Okay, Joshua. Do not go anywhere else. We'll need Ahmed to get ready shortly."

"Yes, Ima."

Chapter 16

Joshua and Ahmed ran down the hallway to Joshua's bedroom. The soiled clothes that Joshua lent Ahmed were folded on a chair near his bed. Ignoring them, he went to his desk drawer and moved objects around quickly. He was searching for something, and Ahmed was curious to find out what it was. Ahmed watched his every move like a cat watching a ball hanging from a string that it has just swatted.

"What are you doing?"

"You'll see, Ahmed. Give me a minute. Where the heck did I put it?"

"Put what, where?" Ahmed kept pushing Joshua to give him an answer.

"Ah, here it is." Joshua walked toward Ahmed and sat down on the bed next to him. "Turn toward me, Ahmed." Joshua opened a box and placed his first soccer medal onto Ahmed's neck.

"What are you doing? Why are you giving this to me, Joshua?"

"This was my first soccer medal ever. I got it when I was seven years old. It was the most exciting day of my life. I want you to wear it and remember me whenever you play soccer."

"Joshua, this is too much. It means too much to you—I can't."

"No, you must, Ahmed. It's the only connection we will have. Please accept it as part of our friendship."

صداقة يديدوت صداقة يديدوت صداقة يديدوت صداقة يديدوت

صداقة يدیدות صداقة يدیدות صداقة يدیدות صداقة يدیدות

Ahmed looked down at the medal, touching the ribbon that held it. He looked at the Hebrew words written on it. "Joshua, I don't want you to take what I'm about to say the wrong way. I just want you to understand. If I wear this medal when I play soccer, I will be considered a traitor, a collaborator of the Israelis. This could even put me and my family in danger. People in my community don't trust one another for the smallest reason, but wearing this would be putting it in their faces. Can you understand what I'm saying? It's not meant to hurt you or insult you. This is the way it is. You know that too."

"I do know and I understand the reality, Ahmed. Sometimes I would just like to put it in the faces of all those who hate and stand up to them and say, 'We're not all like you.' I would never want you to put yourself or your family in danger. What kind of friend would I be just so you could wear some medal of a seven-year-old Israeli boy?"

"Look, I realize what a kind gesture this is giving me such a medal. I will accept it, but you know I can't wear it. I will keep it in my room, hidden in my box of important treasures, and this will be one of them. What do you think? Would that be acceptable to you?"

"That's a great idea. Remember, it's a symbol of our friendship. Friends forever even though we will be some miles apart, okay? Our friendship will be a bond that will remain unbroken."

"Wait. I don't have anything to exchange with you. It can't be one-sided. Let me see what I have. Here, how about my identification papers?" Ahmed laughed as he pretended to hand them over to Joshua.

صداقة يدیدות صداقة يدیدות صداقة يدیدות صداقة يدیدות

"Stop being silly. We don't have much time. What do you have?"

"All right, all right, I'm looking. How about this?" Ahmed held a small photo in his hand. Its edges had been worn with age, and one corner was torn.

"Who is in the photo?"

"Here, I want you to have this. It is a picture of me and my jiddo when I was about five years old. Do you think you'd recognize me?"

"Yeah, you have the same ugly face!" Ahmed pushed Joshua so hard he was teetering on one foot.

"Kidding," Joshua said. "I would absolutely recognize you. It's just a smaller version of you now, but do you want to part with this picture?"

"Listen, Joshua, it's the only thing I have that means something to me, so I want you to have it. Now it's a fair exchange. We've given each other something meaningful." They both held their hands out and shook on it. "It's been an adventure, hasn't it?"

"It sure has, Ahmed, but the best part is that I found a new friend and my Aba has found an old one."

"Joshua," Adiva called out, "it's time for Ahmed to leave. Tell him to gather anything that is his."

"Yes, Ima, I will." They both looked at each other. "Do you have everything?"

"I do. Let's go." They walked down the hallway back to the living room.

Meshek smiled at both. "Shalom, gentlemen. Ahmed, do you have everything? Are you ready to go? Please say your good-byes."

Joshua and Ahmed hugged one last time. Ahmed joined his

صداقة يدّيدوت صداقة يدّيدوت صداقة يدّيدوت صداقة يدّيدوت

parents at the door. Ghali and Barirah thanked Dan and Adiva for a memorable day. Meshek guided Barirah outside, and the soldiers escorted her and Ahmed to the car waiting for them. Ghali turned one more time to Dan while Meshek waited.

"I hope you will sleep well, Dan, when you think of me. Good-bye, my friend." Dan looked at Ghali, trying to understand why he was leaving him with a cryptic message.

Meshek stared at both of them. Dan put his hand on Ghali's shoulder. "Good-bye, Ghali."

Ghali walked down the steps with one of the soldiers who had returned to bring him to the car. Before Meshek turned to join the entourage, he looked into Dan's eyes for several seconds. "Interesting farewell, wouldn't you say?" After saying that, Meshek followed the path to the car. Dan waited until the car drove off.

Adiva stood by the living room doorway. Dan turned to walk back, facing her. "Is everything all right? You look pale."

"Adiva, sit down please." They both sat, and Dan took Adiva's hands into his.

"What is the matter? Tell me. Are you feeling let down because Ghali has left?"

"That's just it, it's what Ghali left me with on the way out. His last words to me were that he hoped I would sleep well when I thought of him. His words gave me a chill. I felt like the person I spent the afternoon with was gone. Meshek eyed me suspiciously with a look that said, 'I told you so.'

"I don't know what to think. I realize many years have passed since we were boys, and our friendship was at another time and on another level. I'm not responsible for what happened to his family.

صداقة يدّيدوت صداقة يدّيدوت صداقة يدّيدوت صداقة يدّيدوت

صداقة يديدوت صداقة يديدوت صداقة يديدوت صداقة يديدوت

We tried to help him as best we could, and Joshua did too. If not for him, Ahmed and his parents may not have been released so soon. This visit would have been a fleeting thought."

"Stop, right now. Ghali and Barirah were very appreciative of what we did for them, and they truly enjoyed the afternoon here as we did too. You have to realize he has been away from you for many years, and he has seen so many things happen in that time between the Israelis and Palestinians. I'm sure those things have changed him in some way, but it seems he still holds the basic values that you say he had as a boy.

"Still, he is not the boy you remember. He is a man who has lived in a world of discontent and hatred for Israel and its existence. Remember, he has also taught his children not to hate and that all people are not troublemakers. You've seen him under strange circumstances. He's lost his family home and was arrested for trying to defend it. These are not the best conditions to meet an old friend. Take comfort in knowing that he is a lot like you in that respect, that he is kind and tolerant. Don't try to create a deeper meaning than what he said to you."

"You are right, Adiva. Mrs. Common Sense, always keeping me from becoming paranoid. You are the level-headed one in this family."

Adiva put her hand on Dan's and kissed him on the cheek. "That's why I'm here, Dan. Now help me clean up please."

They picked up the assorted platters and dishware and put them into the dishwasher. Adiva wrapped up the leftover desserts and placed them in the cupboard. As she put each package away, she realized she had forgotten to give some treats to the Quessems

صداقة يديدوت صداقة يديدوت صداقة يديدوت صداقة يديدوت

صداقة يديدوت صداقة يديدوت صداقة يديدوت صداقة يديدوت

to take on the ride home. There was so much going on, she just couldn't remember everything.

"Joshua," she called.

"Yes, Ima."

"Would you help Aba with the rest of the dishes please?"

"Sure."

"Here, Aba, I'll take those." Joshua brought the remaining cups and saucers and the coffeepot back to the kitchen. He handed them to Ima to rinse and put into the dishwasher. "Can I go to my room now, Ima?"

"Everything completed?"

"Yes it is. Everything is all cleaned up."

صداقة يديدوت صداقة يديدوت صداقة يديدوت صداقة يديدوت

Chapter 17

Joshua walked to his room and sat down on his bed. He was a lot more tired than he thought. The past several days ignited an energy in him that kept him going. The house was now silent, and the energy of Ahmed gone. He felt his body ease down on the bed. Before he knew it, he was drifting off to sleep.

"Ahmed, what is that you're wearing? Doesn't look like Arabic to us, does it guys?" They ganged up on Ahmed, took the ball from him, and threw it to the ground. One of the boys grabbed hold of the medal. "Hebrew? What are you doing with this, Ahmed? Have an Israeli friend we don't know about?" "You don't know what you're talking about," Ahmed shouted. "Leave me alone. I'm free to wear whatever I want." "Not in our territory, Ahmed." Mahmoud pulled on the ribbon, yanking it from Ahmed's neck. He threw it on the ground, and they all began stomping on it. "No, please don't. Joshua, help me. Please. I didn't do anything wrong. He's my friend. Joshua!" "Ahmed, don't let them bully you. Don't, Ahmed."

Joshua woke up from sleep, screaming. Adiva came running. "Joshua, are you all right? What happened?"

"Nothing, Ima. I fell asleep and had a really bad dream. I'm fine."

"Thank goodness. I thought you injured yourself, but you were screaming Ahmed's name."

صداقة يديدوت صداقة يديدوت صداقة يديدوت صداقة يديدوت

"I was probably thinking about him since he left, that's all. Stop worrying. I'm okay."

Adiva left. Joshua sat up. *I don't ever want to put Ahmed in that kind of danger. Please, Ahmed, hide my medal so only you will see it,* Joshua prayed.

He felt sleepy from the last few days and he looked around his room. Games were still on the floor, and there were clothes that needed to be picked up and put in the wash. As he began collecting the pieces of the games, he carefully organized them in their boxes and placed each one on the shelves. He started to collect his clothes and checked his pockets for tissues or any other unwanted object that would interfere with Ima's wash.

Staring at him were the clothes Ahmed had worn before he changed into his own freshly washed ones. Joshua walked over to pick them up. He felt the fabric in his hands and laughed as he thought about the adventure he and Ahmed experienced. He checked the T-shirt pocket, put it in the laundry bag, than moved on to the shorts. He checked the back pockets and found one used tissue.

"Ugh. Sorry, Ahmed, but a dirty tissue from anyone is still disgusting." He took a clean tissue and pulled out the dirty one, throwing it into his wastebasket. Then he felt into the front side pockets. The left one was empty, but when he went into the right pocket, he felt something creased. He unfolded the piece of paper.

"Oh no!" Joshua couldn't believe what he was seeing. It was a picture of young Hamas members with heads covered, holding weapons. He was almost too afraid to turn the page to see what was on the other side, but he had to do it. It was filled with hatred for

صداقة يديدوت صداقة يديدوت صداقة يديدوت صداقة يديدوت

Israel and plans for eradicating it and all the people in it. The flyer was trying to recruit new members with its propaganda. Joshua was devastated and felt deceived.

"It can't be. Ahmed would never align himself with Hamas. I can't believe it. No, someone shoved this in his face, and he had to take it. That's what they do. If he didn't want it, they would start to become suspicious of him, so he took it. He just didn't have time to get rid of it, that's all. No, he forgot it was in his pocket when he left Tulkarm. Yes, that's what happened."

Joshua felt satisfaction in coming up with an explanation for finding this hate-filled literature. Yet he didn't want to get rid of it. He had to keep it, but it had to be kept in a very safe hiding place. His parents could never find it. It would hurt his Aba too deeply. Everything his Aba believed in and taught him would be a lie if he saw the flyer. He would feel betrayed and used by his friend Ghali.

Joshua searched his room for a box, any small box he could find to put the folded paper in it. He opened the drawers of his dresser and found a small ring box that had once held his brother's military ring. Joshua almost put it back, thinking about the irony of using that box to hide a Hamas flyer, but it was all he had. He put it in his pocket and walked out to the courtyard. "I'll be outside for a while, Ima. I just want to get some fresh air."

He walked to a corner of the courtyard where his Ima and Aba couldn't see him; somewhere he knew no one would plant anything. The evening lights were on in the courtyard highlighting a small pindo palm tree. His Ima never planted flowers under the pindo. He knew it would be the perfect spot.

Joshua walked to where it grew. He kneeled on the dirt and

صداقة يديدوت صداقة يديدوت صداقة يديدوت صداقة يديدوت

began digging furiously until he had dug a hole deep enough to bury the box with the folded flyer in it, but not too deep for him to retrieve it.

Keeping a lookout for his parents, he nervously patted the dirt down hard so it would look untouched. Then he wiped his hands on his shorts to remove any excess dirt. He didn't want to bring any attention to himself. He wanted to get to the bathroom and wash his hands and forget what just happened. Staring down at the spot where the flyer lay buried, he whispered to himself, "This will be our secret, Ahmed, a bond never to be broken."

But as Joshua thought about Ahmed going back to Tulkarm and the life he had there, in his heart he knew a friendship between an Israeli and Palestinian boy could only be a breakable bond. Joshua's job had been completed as he walked away from the courtyard and the pindo tree that held his and Ahmed's secret.

صداقة يديدوت صداقة يديدوت صداقة يديدوت صداقة يديدوت

Epilogue

Three years later in Tulkarm, West Bank ...

Eighteen-year-old Ahmed's Abi was accidentally killed walking in the marketplace during a confrontation between Israeli soldiers and a group of young Palestinians. Ahmed Quessem, grieving and angry, has joined Hamas and adopted its political ideology. He is a fervent follower who is being groomed as one of the leading organizers in his village.

At the same time in Netanya, Israel ...

Joshua Atai, also eighteen years old, has enlisted for mandatory service in the Israeli army. He has been assigned to a checkpoint in Netanya, checking documentation of Palestinians trying to enter the city.

صداقة يدِيدوت صداقة يدِيدوت صداقة يدِيدوت صداقة يدِيدوت

To the Israeli and Palestinian people and the hope
for tolerance, respect, and compassion for one
another that they may one day live peacefully.
To my students, who continue to teach me
about the goodness in human beings.
To my father and mother, who taught me to
appreciate beauty in art, music, and theater,
and the most important people in my life—my
husband, Harvey; sons, Adam and Joshua; and my
grandchildren, Layla, Natasha, Vela, and Avi.

IN MEMORY OF ALL THOSE WHO
HAVE LOST THEIR LIVES BECAUSE OF HATRED
AND A PRAYER FOR PEACE IN OUR WORLD.

Acknowledgments

Thank you to Ahmed, who started me on the journey from Tulkarm to Netanya; Doron Matmor from Dog Bytes Computers for his invaluable guidance in helping to keep my story authentic; to Aimee Reff whose expertise made it so easy to begin this book project; and Adriane Pontecorvo, my cheerleader from Archway Publishers, for providing support and encouragement during those times when my momentum waned. My deepest gratitude goes to the Archway staff for their valuable contributions in making my book a reality, and to my son Joshua, for his artistic skills in bringing life to Joshua and Ahmed. My daughter-in-law, Niki, for her magical photography skills.

صداقة يديدوت صداقة يديدوت صداقة يديدوت صداقة يديدوت

It's really amazing when two strangers become best of friends,
but it's really sad when the best of friends become strangers.

CPSIA information can be obtained at www.ICGtesting.com
Printed in the USA
LVOW08*0605170715

446228LV00002B/35/P

9 781480 813861